This book must be returned by the date specified at the time of issue as the DATE DUE FOR RETURN.

The loan may be extended (personally, by post, telephone or online) for a further period if the book is not required by another reader, by quoting the above number / author / title.

Enquiries: 01709 336774

www.rotherham.gov.uk/libraries

CASE OF THE DIXIE GHOSTS

America's bloody Civil War is over, leaving a legacy of bitterness, intrigues and villainy — not all acted out on the American continent. A ship from the past docks in Liverpool, England; the mysterious Mr. Fortune, carrying a burden of secrets, slips ashore and disappears into the fogs of winter. And in London, detective Septimus Dacers finds that helping an American girl in distress plunges him into combat with the Dixie Ghosts, and brings him face-to-face with threatened murder — his own.

A. A. GLYNN

CASE OF THE DIXIE GHOSTS

Complete and Unabridged

LINFORD
Leicester

First published in Great Britain

First Linford Edition
published 2013

A catalogue record for this book is available
from the British Library.

ISBN 978–1–4448–1654–9

Published by
F. A. Thorpe (Publishing)
Anstey, Leicestershire

Set by Words & Graphics Ltd.
Anstey, Leicestershire
Printed and bound in Great Britain by
T. J. International Ltd., Padstow, Cornwall

This book is printed on acid-free paper

Prologue

On an August morning in 1865, sailors on the deck of the merchantman *Barracouta*, of Liverpool, stared open mouthed across the sun smitten waters off the coast of California at the flag fluttering from the high masts of the sleek vessel that had recently come into view and was now drawing closer to their own ship. 'She's built for fast travel and she's armed,' rumbled the *Barracouta's* grizzled bo'sun. 'She has guns fore and aft — but look at her flag and where's she been all these months? Better call the captain.'

When the ship's master appeared on deck, his astonishment matched that of his crew.

'Damned rum business, encountering the like of her,' he exclaimed. 'She's like a ghost out of the recent past. I hope she has no intention of using those guns on us before we parley. She looks uncommon dangerous.'

Soon, the British captain's voice, amplified by a brass speaking trumpet, boomed over the water: 'Ahoy, there! We're the *Barracouta*, out of Liverpool. What ship are you? Your colours intrigue us!'

A tall man among a cluster of uniformed officers aboard the other vessel raised his own trumpet to his lips and answered in a firm voice: 'We're the commerce raider *Shenandoah*. I am Commander James I. Waddell, Navy of the Confederate States of America. I have the honour to command this craft on the active service of that nation'.

The English captain's astonishment echoed in his answer: 'Are you not aware, Commander, that the war between the American states is over? It finished a good three months ago. Have you been off the face of the earth that you do not know it?'

'We have been in arctic waters, destroying Yankee whalers, for a long spell,' replied the American. 'We had word the war was going badly with us some time ago. I trust you are not jesting and it has indeed ended, sir. If so, with what result?'

'I regret to report that the Southern Confederacy was defeated. The North's Mr. Lincoln is dead — assassinated. The old union of states has been restored,' the British captain shouted. 'My nation kept aloof from your internal affairs but I think it right to tell you that the present government of America is calling you people who raided United States' merchant shipping on the high seas a set of pirates. There's every danger of your being executed if you give yourselves up in an American port. For myself, I'd hate to see skilled and brave sailors swinging from the gallows when they believed they were serving their country.'

There was a brief interval of heavy silence then Commander James Waddell replied

'We're aware of what the Yankees think of us, Captain, and I'm obliged to you for your kindly sentiments and for the news, dreadful though it is. You may tell the world that when you met us we were contemplating a bold attack on San Francisco which we heard is poorly defended but we altered course to sail well away from an America where the Union has triumphed at the heavy cost of Southern lives.'

'Where are you bound?' asked the master of the *Barracouta*.

'That's a matter for consultation between my officers and myself but I have a notion your own pleasant land, where I once spent a goodly spell, will be mooted as a good choice.'

'Will you strike your colours, sir?' asked the British captain.

'Never, sir! We doubtless have a long voyage before us but we carry what must be the last Confederate battle flag to fly in the breeze and, by thunder, we'll bear it proudly to whatever port we finally come to rest in.'

The captain of the *Barracouta* gave an appreciative chuckle. 'Your courage does you credit, Commander. May you have a good voyage — and may you not meet any hostile Yankee warships.'

Exactly three months later, after an arduous journey, navigated by her young sailing master, Lieutenant Irvine Bulloch, and cautiously putting in at several ports for a modicum of supplies, the *Shenandoah* approached the mouth of the River Mersey, wreathed by the first of November's fogs.

Off the estuary stood a British warship, *HMS Donegal*. Waddell signalled her and, through her captain, formally surrendered to the British government.

The following morning, escorted by the *Donegal*, the *Shenandoah* docked at Liverpool. It was a kind of homecoming for the vessel. For it was in Liverpool that she started her life as a Confederate raider.

Created for the fast tea run, to bring tea to the British Isles, she was originally named the *Sea King*. Through a combination of finances from wealthy British supporters of the rebel Southern government and that government's most effective and remarkable secret agent, who happened to be the half-brother of Lieutenant Irvine Bulloch, the *Shenandoah*'s sailing master, she was secretly acquired in Liverpool and refitted for the warlike role in which she distinguished herself.

British customs officers came aboard as

Waddell retired to his cabin to write to Lord Russell, Queen Victoria's Foreign Minister, surrendering the vessel, with all her supplies and armaments to the British authorities. A short time later the ship's company gathered on deck for a last time and, in a brief ceremony, the last active Confederate battle flag of the American Civil War was lowered not on the American continent but in Liverpool, half a year after hostilities ceased

Among the ship's officers, keeping low behind a group of taller men was the mysterious little hunchback known only as Mr. Fortune. No one knew anything definite about his background except that he was supposed to be some kind of Confederate official who had slipped away from the capital, Richmond, Virginia, on the fall of the Southern government. He somehow made his way to the Azores and came aboard the *Shenandoah* when she put in there to re-supply. He was suddenly there one morning, visible with the officers among whom he was quartered and who seemed to give him some special respect. He never mingled with the common seamen.

He was not a prepossessing presence, small with his back burdened by a marked hump. His civilian clothing was travel stained but respectable and such as a modest businessman might wear. His face was lean, lantern jawed and that of one used to hard living. Under bushy brows, he had remarkable, glittering eyes. He said little but, when overheard in conversation with the officers, his accent was notably Southern.

Commander Waddell appeared on deck, walking with his characteristic limp caused by a wound received in a duel over an affair of the heart when a young cadet at the U.S. Naval Academy. He was accompanied by his steward who bore a large wooden box out of which the necks of several bottles protruded.

The half dozen British customs officers, who had boarded to check the ship's contents, stood in a row close to the companionway in order to guard against any of the crew slipping ashore and illegally entering the country before being officially recorded.

Waddell gave them a genial nod. 'Gentlemen, we have a small quantity of choice port picked up on our travels,' he announced. 'I trust it will not be seized as contraband.'

The heavily bearded senior customs man matched his geniality.

'Not at all, Commander. It's accepted that a captain may have a quantity of bottled cheer in his keeping for hospitality's sake.'

'Then let hospitality be the word,' said Waddell heartily. 'Will you and your officers join us in a glass to mark such a favourable end to our voyage?'

The customs man shook his head. 'Alas, no, sir. It's against regulations when we're on duty,' he said dolefully.

'Then my officers and the ship's company will drink a toast to your queen who has graciously granted us sanctuary,' Waddell responded. 'Steward, break out the port and the glasses.'

The customs officers snapped rigidly to attention when Waddell raised a full glass and, in the accent of his native North Carolina but as solemnly as any president

8

of a British military mess, intoned: 'Her Britannic Majesty, Queen Victoria!'

The non-drinking customs men chorused: 'Queen Victoria, God bless her!'

They failed to see hunchbacked little Mr. Fortune hastily slip out from the group of officers behind whom he lurked and move under the cover of a deckhouse. Behind their very backs, he nimbly and noiselessly descended the companionway. He disappeared into the dank river mist creeping over the cobbles of Liverpool's cargo cluttered docks.

1

A Lady in Distress

Detective Inspector Amos Twells, of
Scotland Yard, stood outside the vast
oaken doorway set in the forbidding wall
of London's Newgate Prison with Septimus Dacers at his side. He lit his pipe
and blew out copious volumes of smoke
as if trying to fumigate his whole person
after he had endured the prison's foul
atmosphere.

'Well, now you've seen them with
chains on their arms and legs and ticketed
for the Australian boat, you know that
Dandy Jem and Skinny Eustis are out of
our hair for good,' he commented. 'The
colonies underneath the world are welcome to them. I'll admit I regard you as
an interfering busybody, Dacers, as I do
all of you so-called inquiry agents. If you
wanted to be a detective why didn't you
start at the bottom by joining the force

and braving the dangers of the streets as a plodding peeler? But I'll own you did a capital job collaring that ugly pair of swell mobsmen, especially after Jem came close to filleting you with that huge knife. You'd hardly meet a danger as severe as that even if you were a regular policeman.'

Septimus Dacers, tall, lean and clean-shaven in contrast to his companion whose face was fringed by muttonchop sidewhiskers, was a few weeks off his fortieth birthday, but he looked on the slightly older Twells almost as a father figure. He chuckled, knowing that the ever-complaining Twells, while a holy terror to London's wide assortment of villains, had a heart as good-natured as it was lionlike. Twells and his fellow Yard officers might scorn those who set themselves up as private detectives but they had learned that calling on Dacers for occasional assistance was always a worthwhile move.

Twells noted that his chuckling caused Dacers' face to reflect a spasm of pain.

'How are the ribs?' he asked.

'Still bandaged but improving. The

bandages will be off soon. Luckily, the knife didn't really penetrate but I had a bad enough cut along my side.'

'I'd like to shove that knife down Dandy Jem's throat,' growled Twells. 'Still, there's some comfort in knowing they'll put him on a hard enough diet in New South Wales. Did old Lady Caroline Braithwaite slip you a handsome reward for snatching her jewels out of the sticky fingers of the mobsmen?'

'She did very handsomely by me,' said Dacers. 'Very handsomely indeed.'

'That's another thing you fellows have over us', snorted Twells. 'You stand to net a pretty tip as well as a fee where we have to make do with only a policeman's pay.'

Dacers grinned and answered with mock pity: 'Ah, it's such a shame that tipping a peeler can be construed as bribing an officer of the law.'

The pair walked down Newgate Street, which was even gloomier than usual under a leaden sky this late February of 1866. Both men felt the satisfaction of knowing that two of London's most glib-tongued confidence tricksters of the 'swell mobsmen' variety, had been transported for life. They were caught after some sharp detective work, with Dacers aiding the Metropolitan Police, and with some highly dangerous scuffling at its climax.

'What's your next move?' asked Amos Twells.

'To take the omnibus back to Bloomsbury,'

'Where your ever accommodating landlady, Mrs. Slingsby, will doubtless feed you sumptuously then you'll put your feet up while I still have hours of duty before me,' grumbled Twells.

The two parted company with Dacers going in search of the Bloomsbury omnibus, smiling to himself and reflecting that Twells never changed. He would not be content without something to complain about.

The winter evening was drawing in and the first wisps of a threatening fog were beginning to appear in the streets. On the pavements, jostling pedestrians were, as usual, hugging the inner portions of the footways, avoiding the kerbs where the

14

wheels of passing carts and carriages were throwing up gouts of horse foulings. The air was increasingly chilly and Dacers began to look forward to a relaxed evening in warmth and comfort.

When he arrived at the lodgings he had occupied since his first struggling years, he opened the street door to find his landlady, Mrs. Slingsby, waiting in the hall. She was a statuesque widow whose rather severe exterior disguised a tender nature.

'Mr. Dacers, you have a visitor,' she announced. 'A young lady; an American, I think. Miss Roberta Van Trask. I told her I expected you to return fairly early and put her in the parlour rather than have her waiting in your rooms. I made her comfortable with some tea.'

At the mention of the visitor's name, Dacers' eyes widened. 'Miss Van Trask, how surprising,' he said. 'Thank you, Mrs. Slingsby.'

'You know her, then?' said Mrs. Slingsby, her sharp features brightening. She made no secret of her hope that her bachelor lodger would one day find what

15

she called 'a nice wife'.

'I have that honour,' he answered and his landlady's face brightened a little more.

He entered the parlour, hoping none of the unpleasant odours of Newgate Prison lingered about his person and found a woman in her middle twenties, sitting in the usual rather awkward position due to the wide crinoline skirts of the period. She wore a trim velvet jacket and had a small hat on neatly braided black hair. Her attractive, open face would have been more attractive still had she not looked distinctly troubled.

'Miss Van Trask, this is a most unexpected pleasure,' he greeted. 'I'm sorry I was not here when you arrived.'

The girl smiled rather wanly. 'That's all right, Mr. Dacers, your landlady was very kind to me.'

'And how is your father?' Dacers asked, drawing a chair closer to his visitor and sitting down.

'His general health's a great deal better than for some time, though I fear all is not well with him in other respects. I called on you, hoping you can help.'

'I will if I can, you may be sure,'

'Mr. Dacers, I know you can be trusted,' she began, dropping her tone as if frightened of being overheard. 'I knew that quite instinctively when you first came to our home to escort my father on his mission to Liverpool a couple of years ago and, of course, Scotland Yard recommended you to Mr. Adams in the most glowing terms. You looked after my father excellently. He still speaks of you with admiration.'

'And I admire him, Miss Van Trask. It was more than a pleasure to travel with so learned and pleasant a gentleman, even though it was the first time I ever carried a revolver on an assignment.'

'A revolver, yes, that brings me to the reason for my being here,' Roberta Van Trask said. 'I'm sure what I have to tell you will go no further but I am very worried about my father. I fear his position with the diplomatic service of the United States may be in danger.'

Septimus Dacers was surprised. He could hardly imagine that a man so manifestly devoted to his country's well-being as Theodore Van Trask, who held a key position in the United States Embassy under Ambassador Charles Francis Adams, the son of President John Quincy Adams, could endanger his standing through any dereliction of duty. He had escorted Van Trask to the US Consulate in Liverpool on a most urgent mission, on which they carried vital documents and he had taken the measure of the man.

'Tell me more,' he pressed.

'It concerns a visitor my father had a few days ago,' said the girl. 'A rather coarse man and an American — a Virginian. One cannot live in Washington as long as I did without recognising a Virginia accent, Virginia being just across the Potomac River. This man rather pushed his way into our home, demanding to see my father. When my father appeared, he was somewhat frightened and took him into his private room, closed the door and, pretty soon, there was the sound of angry arguing. My father, as you know, had suffered a spell of illness and I became alarmed, fearing he might get too excited, so I intruded, surprising them both.

'The man was standing close to my father quite menacingly and my sudden entry caused him to slip something into the pocket of his coat very hastily but I saw what it was. It was a gun, a Derringer, the same kind of nasty little weapon John Wilkes Booth used to assassinate Abraham Lincoln. I think my father was being threatened with it at the moment I opened the door.'

'Do you know the name of your visitor?' Dacers inquired.

'He announced himself very roughly when he shoved past our butler at the street door. He said he was called Fairfax but I think he was lying. It's an old and honoured Virginia name and it just didn't fit the man. He was obviously no Virginia aristocrat. After my intrusion, he left hurriedly, leaving my father looking very shaken.'

'And did your father tell you anything about the man and the reason for his visit?'

'No. And, ever since, he's been preoccupied and appearing dreadfully worried. He hardly says a word to anyone. He's clearly much disturbed and I fear for both his health and his position. Mr. Adams places the utmost trust in him, as does Mr. Henry Adams, the ambassador's son and private secretary. I'm apprehensive that whatever is worrying him will eventually disturb my father's valuable work at the Embassy.'

Septimus Dacers nodded. He remembered from escorting her father to Liverpool that U.S. Consul Thomas Dudley and his staff there treated Theodore Van Trask with grave respect. Britain was neutral in the American Civil War and Dacers learned nothing of the exact reason for Van Trask's mission to Liverpool. But that port, a major link with America, had played a significant part in the conflict. It was there that the famous Confederate raider *Alabama*, which wrought severe damage on United States' merchant shipping, was built in secret. There, too, the sleek and speedy *Shenandoah*, originally built for the tea trade, was converted into a commerce raider for the Southern rebels. The representatives of Ambassador Adams were constantly trying to track down the elusive agents of the Southern states who organised these menaces to the commerce of the North.

Dacers felt Van Trask's journey from London to the port on the Mersey must be connected to the Union's bugbear of hostile shipbuilding. He remembered how he spotted suspicious looking men lurking around the Liverpool consulate, obviously noting the comings and goings of persons. They frequently displayed signs of transatlantic origins: a hat with a broader brim than usual in England; a pair of American square toed boots or evidence of addiction to chewing tobacco, an American habit almost unknown in Britain. Doubtless, these were agents of the Southern Confederacy, keeping an eye on their enemy's nerve centre in Britain. He tried to recall the appearance of some of them but could not remember any resembling the one the girl spoke of.

'This man who was threatening your

father, Miss Van Trask, what was he like? Did he have any distinguishing marks?' he asked. 'I take it you'd know him again.'

'I certainly should. He was tall and powerfully built with a heavy moustache rather blonde in colour and there was one very noticeable thing about him — he had a blue mark, what I think is called a powder burn, near his right eye.'

'You mean the kind of thing soldiers sometimes have, caused by the flashback of the breech of a musket when it's aimed from the shoulder?'

'Yes, he looked as if he might have been a soldier at some time, but not an officer. He smelt of whisky and his manner was disgustingly uncouth. That's why his name of Fairfax didn't ring true. A genuine Fairfax would certainly be a Southern officer and they pride themselves on their gentlemanly courtesy. I have to concede that point though I was opposed to their cause in the late war but this man had nothing of the Southern officer about him.'

Dacers smiled slightly. 'Well observed, Miss Van Trask,' he praised. 'London's a big place and finding one man in it is no easy task but at least this fellow has characteristics to mark him out in a crowd if you want me to find him and make him answer for his actions.'

The girl sighed. 'To tell you the truth, Mr. Dacers, I'm in a dilemma and scarcely know what I want. My greatest desire is to see my father free of this worry and never to be bothered by an armed ruffian barging in on him again. I keep remembering how, on the day Mr. Lincoln was shot, one of the conspirators charged into the sickroom of Mr. Seward, the Union's Secretary of State, and tried to kill him in his bed. I fear something of that kind because these men have something against him and it must be something political. At the same time, I do not want Mr. Adams, or his son, Mr. Henry Adams, or any of the Embassy staff to get wind of the affair. Nor does my father, who is fearful of anyone connected to the Embassy getting to know.'

Roberta Van Trask sighed again, leaned forward and, after biting her lip as if in doubt about revealing something and dropping her tone yet lower, said: 'You see, in the very strictest confidence, I fear my father is mixed up in something. Or, at least, unscrupulous people have entangled him in some intrigue. The Embassy must never know of it, nor the official British police. My father's illness a couple of years ago weakened him considerably and I worry that if this mysterious affair, whatever it is, creates a public scandal it could even cause his death. I came to you because when I first met you I formed the opinion that you are a truly honest and honourable man and my father holds the same opinion. I feel you're the one man in London who can help relieve my dreadful anxiety and, more importantly, my father's troubles.'

'I could never see Mr Van Trask involved in intrigue and certainly not in anything damaging to the United States,' Dacers said.

She shook her head. 'Mr. Dacers, you do not know Washington — especially the Washington of those years when civil war was raging. There were plots and counter-plots, divided loyalties, spying, counter-spying and every shade of treason. I remained there when my father was posted to England because I had a good position in the Treasury Department.

'My father became ill in 1863 so, since my mother is dead, I resigned and came here to help in nursing him but my years in Washington gave me an insight into much double dealing and trickery. Civil war is a terrible thing. It seems to bring out the worst, even in people who are normally honest, loyal and trustworthy.

'America was a divided house, remember, and in such a place many people and what they do and say are often not what they appear. It was easy to quite inadvertently make an enemy and fall into some dangerous situation. I fear that something of the kind has happened to my father.'

Septimus Dacers considered that point for a moment then said: 'But he has not been in Washington for a long time.'

'We hear that, since the death of Mr. Lincoln, things are even worse in Washington,' said Roberta Van Trask.

'Chickens are coming home to roost and all kinds of revenge are being taken. New and often grotesque rumours are flying about, mostly concerning the actions of people during the war. One says high-ranking people in the North were profiteering through illegal trade with the rebel South; another says Mr. Lincoln's assassin, through an elaborate plot was not killed by soldiers after fleeing into Virginia and is alive somewhere in Europe. Yet another makes the unbelievable claim that the Northern Secretary of War, Mr. Stanton, was in the plot to kill the President.'

'So you think perhaps some new and damaging tale about your father has been concocted in the swamp of intrigue that is post war Washington?' inquired Dacers.

'Yes, and I worry that these men might continue to harass him to either his ruination or his death,' she said with a half suppressed sob.

'Miss Van Trask, on two occasions, you referred to 'these men'. Does that mean there were others in this attack on your father besides the fellow calling himself Fairfax?'

'Two others certainly accompanied him but did not enter the house,' she said. 'When he left my father after my intrusion, he ran for the street door and was pursued by our butler, who is elderly and not very agile. I attempted to follow too, but,' she indicated her wide hooped crinoline, 'a woman simply cannot run in today's fashions. He flung the door open and got clean away. There was a brougham, a closed carriage waiting outside the house. At the reins was a man bundled up in heavy clothing and with his hat obscuring his face. Fairfax leapt into the carriage and there was a third man inside who helped him through the door. I caught only a brief glimpse of him before the driver whipped up the horse and they sped away but I have a strange feeling that I've seen that third man before, a long time ago although I can't think where. He was small and, for a moment, he looked at me with notably glittering eyes. I had the impression that he was a hunchback.'

'So,' Dacers mused, 'we have your big man with a blonde moustache and a powder burn who takes a drink of whisky; one who might be a hunchback and a driver who, like most coachmen in these winter days, looks like nothing but a bundle of clothing. If I locate these fellows, what can I do? You do not want the police involved but I have no powers of arrest. I certainly want to help you but, at best, I could only warn them off with the threat of police action; after all, this so-called Fairfax did commit trespass and threatening behaviour. But a warning might not be enough. A fellow who makes free with a Derringer pistol sounds like a desperate customer and he might prove tenacious and show up again. There are a few haunts in London where I might find a lead on this crew. I'll do what I can.'

Roberta Van Trask gave him a hesitant smile. 'If that is the best you can do and it offers some hope of success, then please do it. I'll be grateful for anything that might take this terrible burden off my father's shoulders,' she said.

'Very well, Miss Van Trask. Tell me, you

arrived here unescorted. How did you travel?'

'By cab. Normally, I would have my maid, Esther, accompany me but I wanted to see you strictly in private. Although Esther is completely trustworthy, I did not want my father or anyone from the embassy to know I came to consult you.'

'Then let me escort you as far as the cab stand at the corner of the square and see you safely on your way. Not that I think you are a young lady who is easily frightened but our ugly friends could have been watching your home and might have followed you.'

The American girl squared her shoulders and set her jaw decisively. 'I assure you I am not easily frightened,' she declared firmly. 'I'll stand my ground against any threat to my father but I'm obliged to you for your courtesy.'

An admiring smile crossed Dacers' usually grave face and she noticed how boyish it suddenly made him appear.

It was now fully dark outside and, after he had seen her safely off in a cab, Dacers paced homeward through the evening gloom thinking of the narrative he had heard. There was something deep and potentially dangerous in the happenings at the home of the American diplomat and, only for the fact that police involvement might spark off the public scandal Roberta Van Trask feared, he would have liked to acquaint Twells with the matter.

'It's the sort of case old Amos would grab with both hands,' he muttered to himself. 'I'm not at all sure where to begin or where it will take me, but a lady in distress must be helped, so some sort of start must be made.'

2

Dark Places: Dark Deeds

Dacers walked out early the following morning after a night in which confused scraps of dreams containing pictures of Roberta Van Trask, various threatening men and scenes from the war in America chased themselves through his slumbers. He breakfasted then decided on a stroll to clear his head and think about the matter the American girl had placed before him the evening before.

The fog had cleared and, as usual, the streets were alive early. Vehicles of all kinds from brewery wagons to the light donkey carts of costermongers and from rumbling, crowded omnibuses to more elegant carriages crowded the roads. On the footways, throngs of clerks, char-women, milliners and brisk, impatient men of business, as usual, elbowed and shoved each other, hastening to get to work on time and showing the lack of neighbourly consideration, characteristic of London at rush hour. The sooty form of the sweep, trailed by the even sootier apparition of his boy, laden with brushes, moved among them; milkmen decanted the day's supply of milk in the areas of Bloomsbury's substantial houses then bellowed the traditional: 'Milk below!' for the benefit of the cook and kitchen maids. On a street corner, a policeman was trying to mediate between an irate pedestrian who claimed he had almost been run over and a carter who protested his innocence with the shouts of all three mounting while a ragged old man, hoping to cadge a penny, wailed an almost unrecognisable hymn which set a stray dog howling in a similar morose tone.

As Dacers turned into Russell Square, which was no more tranquil than anywhere else at that hour, old Setty Wilkins came to mind. Enigmatic old Setty was often worth consulting. There was no telling what might emerge from the aged man's brimming vault of London knowledge so Dacers turned his footsteps towards Seven Dials.

In that tangled and insalubrious region, he came to a short street hemmed in by rickety property, some of it half-timbered and dating from centuries before. Over the door of a tumbledown structure, a roughly lettered board announced: '*Seth Wilkins, Practical Engraver*'. Dacers approached the door over a surface of broken cobbles and stagnant puddles.

Inside his shadow haunted workshop, Setty Wilkins lifted a small copper plate from an acid bath with metal tongs, shook off surplus acid then pushed the end of his nose close to the plate, screwed up his eyes and inspected the etching he had just completed. Setty was well trained in his trade and, in lines bitten into the metal was the neat depiction of a woman suspended from the hangman's gallows. The old man gave a grunt of satisfaction.

'That'll be capital on a confession fakement come the next time some fair beauty dances the Paddington frisk on the gallows in front of Newgate,' he rumbled to himself. He meant the plate would produce an illustration for a totally spurious 'last true confession' of the gallows' victim, hawked through the bawling, brawling crowd that flocked to public hangings and made gala occasions of them. The 'confession' would be what the criminal fraternity called a 'fakement,' a piece of sheer fiction, produced for a pittance by some gin-ruined unfortunate employed by a printer of penny broadsheets.

Ancient Setty Wilkins turned his hand to many shifts to get his living. These days, he was a good deal more legitimate than in years gone by but it was said that he once risked the Newgate gallows himself by forging banknotes.

The door of the workshop darkened and Setty looked up to see the tall, lean form of Septimus Dacers entering.

'Vy, Mr. Dacers, as ever was!' he greeted heartily. 'I 'eard Dandy Jem nearly croaked you with the blade of his snickersnee an' now they're makin' an Australian farmer of 'im. Not before time. I allus said he didn't have brains enough to keep clear of either the hangman or

Botany Bay for long.' Small, wizened and gnome-like Setty was of indeterminate age and his jargon, tellingly, was largely the criminal 'cant' of the previous reign of King William the Fourth, which, around 1830, was replaced by a new underworld language to baffle the 'New Police', just created by Sir Robert Peel. He had the reversed v's and w's of previous generations of Cockneys.

The character of London was stamped all over him and he possessed an almost uncanny knowledge of the city's obscurest corners and of its myriad inhabitants. He cocked his head to one side and surveyed Dacers critically then declared: 'You ain't lookin' so bad arter a mill with Dandy Jem an' I 'opes you're as good as I sees you.'

'I'm quite well, Setty, and improving every day, thank you,' said Dacers.

'Come, now, Mr Dacers,' responded Setty with a change of tone, 'you vants somethin', otherwise you vouldn't be honourin' me vith a wisit, vould you, old culley?'

'You're shrewd as ever, Setty,' grinned

Dacers. 'I'm looking for a hint or two.'

'Not on behalf of the crushers, I 'opes,' said Setty, narrowing his eyes. ' Though he professed to be in a reformed condition, he still regarded the peelers as more a public menace than a benefit.

'No, you may be sure the police are not involved.'

'Good. Got to take care. A man never knows vots's vot these days. So, if it's information you're arter, vot are you vontin' to know?'

'Where do Americans congregate in London?'

'Vell, the American Church, Tottenham Court vay, if you means square-rigged, prim an' proper Americans but, knowin' your trade, I suppose you don't. I expect it's Americans more rough around the edges you mean.'

'Two I can identify and there's a third I can't, a carriage driver who might not be an American. I don't know how you do it but you seem to know what's going on all over London though you hardly ever leave Seven Dials, you old rogue.'

'There's one gaff that's always gathered

a crew of different nationalities, Yankees included,' Setty Wilkins said. 'The Blue Duck pub at Chandler's Stairs beside the river, 'ard by Hungerford Bridge. It's a pretty low boozing-ken. Could be the place to try.'

'Thanks, Setty, only this pair would object to being called Yankees,' Dacers replied.

Setty Wilkins gave him a crooked grin. 'So it's got something to do vith the big rumpus in America and the bunch that fought the Yankees — the coves from Dixie, as I 'ear they calls it? I heard there was some of that sort lurkin' around the Blue Duck.'

''Nuff said,' responded Dacers. 'I suppose the place is at its liveliest at night?'

'Of course, and it can be no end of a rough shop. So remember that wound you got off Dandy Jem. Watch your step, old culley.'

Dacers left Setty's lair and crossed the broken cobbles again thinking of the old man's parting observation and a sudden cold logic took hold of his mind. Here he was, with a strapped up knife wound and, while unarmed himself, was seeking one man known to go armed and two others whose potential for trouble was unknown. Why? To deliver a feeble message that they had best behave themselves or the police would be informed. All at once, the whole project appeared ludicrous.

He recalled Roberta Van Trask's troubled face and the appeal in her eyes as she sought his help. It really was a matter for the regular police but he had volunteered the limited assistance he could offer, hardly giving a thought to anything but the girl's beauty and her distress. It was as if he had been mesmerised into it. Then he wondered if he was falling in love with Miss Van Trask.

Dacers, ran his thoughts, *Amos Twells had the measure of you when he called you an interfering busybody and you certainly are a damned fool of a busybody who fancied himself a dashing knight in shining armour. You might be blundering into something that'll end with you suffering much more than a swell mobsman's knife wound.*

Then his inborn chivalry took hold of him as he recalled the way the girl squared her shoulders and displayed her determination to defend the reputation of her father. He believed Theodore Van Trask to be as honest and devoted a servant of his country as any man and he was being wronged in some unspecified way. So what could an Englishman who abhorred the use of guns and who did not own one himself do but take her side — even if it meant recklessly going up against men with the famous transatlantic penchant for firearms?

Consequently, when another February evening descended and river mists were creeping up from the malodorous Thames, he made his way to the vicinity of Hungerford Bridge and the Blue Duck tavern. Garbed to visit the hostelry described by Setty Wilkins as 'no end of a rough shop', he was in a working man's suit of fustian with a muffler and a greasy woollen cap. The labourer's obligatory short clay pipe drooped from his mouth.

Old Setty Wilkins seemed rarely to leave his engraving shop but it was as if, like some wizard concealed in a cave, he could send his disembodied spirit forth to wander in every region of the great city, even its murkiest and dangerous nooks and corners, discovering all manner of goings on. When Setty gave Dacers a tip, it usually proved worth following and Dacers felt his usual confidence in the old man's tip concerning the Blue Duck.

It meant searching the margin of the River Thames where a huge sewer laying project and the creation of a vast riverside improvement was under way. Old buildings had been torn down and many more were in process of demolition. There was a confusion of temporary sheds, builders' machinery and piles of construction material around the base of Hungerford Bridge, recently reconstructed to replace one designed by the ingenious Isambard Kingdom Brunel.

He wandered through this dark and entangled scenery and eventually found the Blue Duck in a dogleg of a lane leading down to the river. He heard it before he saw it. A fiddle was scraping and there was a harsh roaring of a music

40

hall song: *Champagne Charlie*. The building was another huddled relic of a much earlier age, as were so many in London's riverside region. Feeble yellow lamplight did its best to struggle out of dirty windows.

He moved out of the way as two tattered figures, one with an arm around the other's shoulder, lurched out of the door warbling in unsure unison:

'*Champagne Charlie is me name,*
'*Champagne drinkin' is me game,*
'*I'm the idol of the barmaids*
'*Champagne Charlie is me name*'

Entering the den, Dacers glanced up to read the name of the licensee on the lintel: '*Josiah Tooley, Licensed to retail Beer, Porter, Spirits and Tobacco*' and he pushed open a creaking door, allowing a tide of raucous din to gush out. Inside, partially enveloped in a pall of tobacco smoke, was a jostle of roughly clad men, some labourers, some seamen, many obviously foreign, and river boatmen mixed in with garishly gowned, painted

41

women, plainly 'dollymops', operated by the madams of riverside houses of joy. Fiddle and bellowing lungs continued the song.

He pushed his way through the crowd to the bar lined with loungers. Behind it, sweated two barmen under the direction of a bald and obese man with a red face, clearly Mr Tooley.

It was from the landlord that Dacers ordered a glass of grog while aware of mistrusting glances from those lining the bar and from Tooley himself. A stranger, even one matching much of the clientele in dress, did not go unnoticed at the Blue Duck, it seemed.

Tooley pushed the mixture of rum and water across the counter and, over the din of the customers' roaring a new song, addressed Dacers with point blank inquisitiveness: 'Not your usual port of call, this gaff, is it?' His voice was heavy with suspicion, which was also reflected in his small eyes.

'No,' said Dacers. 'Just looked in thinkin' I might spot a cove I'm acquainted with. Seems he might come in here now and again.' There was an authentic touch to his mock Cockney.

'Not a disguised peeler are you?' asked Tooley, point blank again.

Dacers gave a dismissive laugh mingled with a touch of scorn. 'Not any kind of peeler and never likely to be but I'm lookin' for a big bloke, American with a fair moustache. Matter of business,' he tapped the side of his nose. The gesture, indicating business of a most private and personal nature, was readily understood by Josiah Tooley.

'I see,' said he. 'I just don't want the scandal of an arrest in here. It could give the place a bad name an' that 'ud be a real disgrace.'

Dacers slyly took in the tough, drunken and shifty looking patrons and the over-painted dollymops. 'I s'pose you're right', he replied without batting an eye.

Tooley said: 'Can't say I knows this bloke you mention, but there's lots come in here at different times and I can't remember 'em all. It's a very popular house, y'see. An' very respectable, like I just told you.'

'I sees that,' confirmed Dacers, stone faced.

Behind Dacers' back, just visible beyond a phalanx of standing drinkers, hooting a boozy chorus, the door opened and two men entered. One was tall, heavily built and with a fair moustache. His companion was shorter, stocky and with a pugnacious face under a billycock hat of the style favoured by the horse racing community. Josiah Tooley, looking past Dacers, noticed them and suddenly said: 'Well, I hopes you find your man but I think you've been misinformed. He don't sound like anyone who comes in here, 'Scuse me, I have to do things.'

He walked along the area at the back of the bar, moving remarkably quickly for one so corpulent, slipped out into the crowd of drinkers. He made directly for the pair who had just entered and were beginning to negotiate a passage through the throng of imbibers.

Dacers was still facing the bar and Tooley made urgent gestures to the two men, indicating that they should turn and head back to the door. In a tone just

44

audible over the din of the singers, he warned: 'Get out! Bloke at the bar's snoopin'. Asked about you. Get out, quick.'

The pair turned, quickly strode to the door and exited with Tooley following. Out in the cold air, the man with the fair moustache asked in a slow drawl representative of the Southern American states: 'Is he from over the pond?'

'No, an Englishman, dressed up in a fustian suit and black cap. Says he ain't a crusher but I ain't so sure. If he is one, he ain't going to say so, is he? He's got the style of a regular working cove but them detectives is smart at acting. You told me to warn you if anyone came asking about you, Mr. Fairfax.'

'Thanks, Josh. He's fishy, all right. We ain't expecting anyone to look in on us. We'll make his acquaintance in due course. We'll maybe give him a little persuading to mind his own business.'

'Don't be too hasty, Cal,' cautioned the pugnacious man in the billycock in a drawl similar to his companion's. 'Maybe we should just blow out of here quietly.

We could be laying up a heap of trouble for ourselves if he's from the police.'

'That's right. Watch what you're about,' hissed Tooley in a sudden panic. 'If he is a peeler and you croak him or injure him, I'll have every crusher in London charging in on me!' He retreated back to the door and gave a last anxious warning before entering: 'Remember, if you gives him a towelling, don't do it anywhere near my gaff!'

Tooley slipped back into the rowdy depths of his drinking den where Septimus Dacers, was still facing the bar, absorbing the sight of the assorted humanity crammed into the smoky confines of the Blue Duck.

There was a scattering of races and colours; men from the open sea and others whose variety of boats rode the Thames; a few soldiers in scarlet tunics and gin-sodden men in tatters from the lower depths of the city, mostly slumped over the tables. Dollymops in borrowed plumes belonging to their bawdy house mistresses sat on the knees of leering drunks or canoodled with them in corners. All not otherwise engaged roared a hoarse chorus of another popular song the sweating fiddler was grinding out, *The Ratcatcher's Daughter:*

> *'Her pa caught rats*
> *And she sold sprats*
> *All round and about that quarter;*
> *And all the gentlefolk thereabout*
> *Loved the pretty little Ratcatcher's*
> *daughter.'*

* * *

Every Tom, Dick and Harry's in the place except the one I'm looking for, thought Dacers, unaware that the man he sought and his companion had entered the premises and were shooed away by Tooley. He reflected on how stupid he was to put faith in Setty Wilkins as in some sort of oracle. How on earth could Setty, living in Seven Dials as a near recluse, know anything of what went on down here near Hungerford Bridge? He concluded that, probably Josiah Tooley told him the truth when he said the man

Dacers sought was unknown in the Blue Duck and it would be fruitless to stay there any longer.

He finished the fiery tasting grog, turned and pushed his way through the standing mass of drinkers and headed for the door.

As he came out of the tavern there was a brief blossoming of lamplight from the door, which illuminated him. Two bulky black figures, crouching just out of the ambit of the light, stirred and there was a whispered sentence: 'That's him — fustian suit and black cap!'

Before Dacers realised that a couple of men were lurking close to the door, there was a sudden scuffle of boots and a pair of heavy bodies came lunging out of the shadows, barging into him and almost knocking him off his feet, sending his breath gusting out of him. The aggression of the man who called himself Fairfax had won out over the caution of the one in the billycock.

Dizzy with the notion that a veritable avalanche of human bodies had fallen on him, Dacers nevertheless perceived by the dim light that the larger of the two had a moustache, probably fair in colour. *Fairfax!* he thought as his senses reeled.

Two pairs of hands grabbed his clothing and he was shoved backwards on his heels, with a force that caused the healing knife wound in his side to jab a sharp pain through his ribs. Within the Blue Duck, the drinkers began to bawl another music hall favourite, the rollicking *Villikins and His Dinah*, as an incongruous accompaniment to the violence being enacted outside.

Gasping and grimacing, Dacers was slammed against the wall of the pub and held there. One of his attackers gave off a strong odour of whisky mingled with tobacco and, from the one whose dark silhouette was topped by the shape of a billycock hat, there was the distinct aroma of horses. While he tried desperately to regain his breath, his mind began to clear and he remembered the coachman who drove away from the American Embassy. He had almost forgotten about him. So Roberta Van Trask and her father were indeed menaced by three adversaries: the man who called himself Fairfax, the mysterious one who might be a hunchback and the fellow who was the bundled up coachman the day Fairfax intruded on Theodore Van Trask.

Dacers managed to lift a knee and jab it into the midst of the dark, combined bulk of his assailants who were forcing him against the damp bricks of the wall.

He ground it into a groin, was rewarded with an anguished, snarling obscenity and was then pushed against the wall even more forcefully.

Something round and hard was clapped against his temple. *Fairfax's Derringer!* he thought.

'You goddam nosy Limey!' growled a voice almost in his ear. 'What are you snoopin' around for? Our business is none of your concern. I've a mighty notion to blow your interferin' brains out.' There was something slightly crazed about the voice, as if the man was on the edge of hysteria. Then the weapon was pressed harder against Dacers' temple. 'By God, I *will*. I'll blow a hole in your head and toss your corpse into the river.'

'Go easy, Cal,' cautioned the second man. 'Don't go off your head again. If you shoot and he's a copper, all hell will be let loose. All our plans could be jimmied.'

'What the hell do we care? Tomorrow, we'll be in Cardsworth, seein' this Vaillant lord or knight or whatever damn fool Limey title he has. You know what they say about the Thames, sometimes bodies are never found and, anyway, we'll be well clear of London in a couple of weeks.'

'Hush up! You're blabbin' too much,' said his companion firmly. 'You know damned well Fortune warned you against that time and again.'

When Fairfax spoke of firing, Dacers had almost automatically stopped struggling, frozen under the ominous threat of the firearm clapped against his temple. He began again to wriggle and shove against the combined weight of his assailants, taking advantage of what appeared to be divided opinion between the two, which was staying Fairfax's trigger finger. He noticed that the marked edge of hysteria in Fairfax's voice had intensified and he memorised the names he had mentioned: somewhere called Cardsworth, someone with a title named Vaillant and someone called Fortune.

'Quit squirming, goddam you!' exploded Fairfax. 'Quit squirming while I put a bullet into your brain.'

'No, Cal!' objected the other. 'I keep telling you: shoot him and, if he's a copper, it'll raise holy hell and Fortune will pull the guts out of you if our operation is ruined!'

Even in the midst of the physical struggle and with the swirling turmoil of his senses, Dacers felt there was something different about this man. Seeming to be as much a ruffian as his companion, he nevertheless gave the impression of having to constantly impart some common sense into Fairfax as if he was frightened of his companion going too far in his strongarm actions.

The pressure of the pistol was lifted from Dacers' head and Fairfax said: 'All right, we've been hanging around here for too long and the place is too damned public. I'm knocking him cold and slinging him in the river. He can take his chances there.'

There was a sharp cry of objection from the other man, which was cut short for Dacers as something crashed down on the crown of his head. As his consciousness reeled then sank into a black gulf, he tried to ensure he remembered the names he had heard: *Cardsworth* and *Vaillant* and there was a third one — *Fortune*.

3

Discoveries in The Country

Dacers came to, lying on soft, muddy ground. His nostrils were filled with a stench all Londoners knew only too well: the sickening reek of the mighty River Thames. His head ached abominably, the knife wound in his side throbbed and, for a few confused moments, he thought he had been cast into the river and was lying on its bed. He rose to his knees, tried to accustom his eyes to the blackness of the night and realised that he was on the edge of the Thames.

For untold generations, the river was little more than an open sewer, into which spilled the city's raw sewage. It spread both what Londoners knew as 'the great stink' and recurring epidemics of deadly cholera. For almost a decade, however, vast improvements were in hand, steered by the brilliant engineer Joseph Bazalgette, whose ingenious system of sewers would give the city a cleaner bill of health. Additionally, the many great tracts of filthy mud at the margins of the river were cleared and built over with the wide and handsome embankments that would become a feature of the city.

Some mud flats, such as those in the vicinity of Chandler's Stairs and the Blue Duck were still unimproved. Septimus Dacers realised he had been dumped on one of these.

He fumbled around, trying to locate his cap but was unsuccessful. He felt his tousled hair gingerly and discovered a large bump and presumed Fairfax hit him with his Derringer. He had been lying face down and the front of his clothing was wet and covered with malodorous river mud. He had no idea of the time. The night was black, without a moon and starless. In the distance, he could hear the subdued noise of the city, which never truly slept.

Stumbling, trying to find his feet and anxious to be clear of the noxious miasma of the river, he swerved to his left, realising that, from the sounds, the city lay that way. He crossed tracts of mud and puddles, eventually found a low wall, struggled to climb it and discovered he was in a dark laneway. He sat on the wall, recovering his breath and trying to straighten his thoughts into a logical sequence then he heard a swift *clip-clop* of hoofs.

Out of the darkness came a light donkey cart as favoured by the coster-mongers, London's street traders in fruit and vegetables. The meagre light was sufficient to show Dacers that stick-thin man at the reins was every inch a coster in a hard wearing jacket embellished with rows of pearl buttons, a cap with a large peak and, about his neck, the Cockney coster's pride, a 'kingsman' — a colourful silk kerchief. Dacers' uncertain eyesight discerned a lean face and a pair of eyes lit by humour under the peaked cap. The coster halted the donkey.

'What-ho, culley?' he greeted cheerfully. 'Night on the beer? Got into a muddle an' fell into a puddle? Done it meself many a time, specially arter a

Punch an' Judy of a row with me old gal. You're properly three sheets in the wind. Where are you tryin' to steer for?'

'Bloomsbury,' mumbled Dacers.

'Bloomsbury — easily done!' chuckled the coster. 'Can't have you wanderin' the town cuttin' that figure. Peelers 'ud collar you for drunk and incapable. Cart's empty, jump in. I'm bound for the market to catch the early mornin' rush. Can drop you within easy reach of Bloomsbury, right as ninepence. Glad to help a fellow sufferer out, old culley. Me old gal plays Old Harry with me if I have an extra bottle or two.'

Hardly able to believe his good fortune, Dacers climbed into the empty cart with some difficulty and gratefully laid himself down on rough boards which gave off a mingled aroma of potatoes and cabbages. The driver set the donkey off at a smart trot and Dacers closed his eyes and recollections of events in the last few hours swirled through his head.

He felt he had behaved like a halfwit as all his earlier apprehension about his mission returned. Going off to warn anyone who was such a desperado as to carry a firearm that he had best behave himself or the police would be alerted seemed from the start like scolding a misbehaving child but he had taken that course — or, rather, had plunged into it without adequate thought. Thanks to his almost juvenile good intentions, he had, in the common language of the streets, made a 'guy' of himself.

Facing Roberta Van Trask and hearing her story, he felt he would do anything for such a girl. So his 'anything' for his lady in distress consisted of blundering into the clutches of a pair of ruffians; coming close to having his brains blown out; receiving a beating and a severe crack on the head and being dumped in the stinking Thames mud. To the trotting of the donkey and the creaking of the cart, he wondered if he was truly smitten by the American girl and if all his vicissitudes were the price of love?

Then a more prosaic line of thought took over. Not knowing how, behind his back, Josiah Tooley had warned the two Americans of his presence and shooed them out of the Blue Duck, he wondered how the pair came to be lying in wait for him at the door. Then he recalled that he visited the Blue Duck following Setty Wilkins' tip. When he came to think of it, Setty was the only person other than Roberta Van Trask who knew he was seeking men who had something to do with the recent civil war in America.

Setty was an enigma. Supposed to have lived a criminal's life in the long ago, he was now reformed. He was full of strange and varied knowledge of the darkest London affairs though he seemed rarely to leave cramped and squalid Seven Dials. He was certainly deep as a well, but was he somehow mixed up in the menace from across the Atlantic that threatened the diplomat Theodore Van Trask? And had he steered Dacers into a trap? No, that was unthinkable. Dacers had known him for a long time and, with his astonishing knowledge, he had proved more than useful and thoroughly trustworthy.

The coster went out of his way to reach the edge of Bloomsbury and obligingly dropped Dacers close enough to home for him to make only a short journey through the streets, now beginning to lighten under a rather leaden dawn. He arrived at his lodgings without incident, put his key silently into the street door, crept into the hall, taking care not to make any noise to waken Mrs. Slingsby or Emma, her maid.

He went to his bedroom as silently as he could, collected his night clothes and made a journey to the basement where there was a hip-bath and a copper for heating water. Working as silently as he could, he prepared a hot bath, shed his soiled clothing, examined his wound, finding that its healing condition had not been interfered with despite the wrenching it received in the tussle at the Blue Duck. He quickly but thoroughly bathed in the hip-bath.

Then, in his night attire and carrying his muddied clothing, he silently mounted the stairs for his bedroom and slept soundly until the dawn blossomed into day.

Always an early riser, Dacers was up at his usual time though, after his exploits of the previous night, his mattress seemed to have acquired magnetic powers over his body.

Mrs. Slingsby noted the signs of his recent ill-usage in the form of bruises here and there on his face, but he had been under her roof for over a decade and she knew his calling as a private inquiry agent frequently led him into rough company. She had learned to make no comment though she had known some anxious moments, as when he recently received his severe knife wound. That morning, she saw evidence of someone having taken a bath in the basement during the night and all the signs pointed to her lodger being involved in another of his 'business affairs' into which she never inquired. She only hoped he would come out of them safely.

After breakfasting, Dacers spent a little time looking up some reference works in the small library he kept in his room.

In a directory of Great Britain's landed and titled gentry, he found:

'*Vaillant, Sir Oswald Hector, Knight*'. There followed details of his age — he was 60 — education, marriage, and a list of business concerns with which he held directorships or was otherwise associated. Three took Dacers' immediate interest: *'Partner, British-American Cotton Exporting Co., Savannah, Georgia; Partner, Transatlantic Steam Shipping Partnership, Liverpool; Director, Rockwell-Mersey Shipbuilders, Birkenhead'* . . . and, after details of his various clubs, there followed his address: *'Fairwinds Manor, Cardsworth, Hertfordshire.'*

In a gazetteer, he found: *'Cardsworth: Hamlet, Hertfordshire, England; largely agricultural; 1 mile from township of Tringford on London-northwest railway line, Euston . . . '*

Next, with sharpened interest, he consulted Bradshaw's Railway Guide and found that while the service between London and Cardsworth was regular and frequent throughout the day, the first train from Euston station did not leave until almost 10 a.m. and it was still only a quarter to nine.

Dacers made a quick decision, went to his room and changed into a tweed suit and stout boots and selected a low crowned hat. Downstairs, he told his Mrs. Slingsby that he would be away for the greater part of the day.

A brisk walk by way of Russell Square and Woburn Place brought him to Euston Station, the first railway station to be built in London. He passed under its heavy Doric arch and entered the architect's proud triumph: the great hall of Euston, a vast, high ceilinged cathedral of the great steam age. It was crowded and bustling as usual with every description of passenger accompanied by every kind of baggage and the constant hissing and growling of locomotives issued from the direction of the platforms.

Tall-hatted railway policemen prowled among the throng with eyes alert for luggage snafflers and pickpockets and a store of harsh words for the match sellers, hurdy-gurdy players and common cadgers who haunted the place. He noticed that two constables were studiously watching a trio of overdressed loungers — swell mobsmen, chancers who practised sophisticated dodges and the brethren of Dandy Jem and Skinny Eustis, now *en route* to Australia.

Pushing his way through the crowd, he made for the window where tickets were dispensed and when he was in sight of it, he saw two men walking away from it obviously having just bought tickets. They had the look of businessmen in dark frock coats and stovepipe hats. Each carried a dispatch case. One was taller than the other with a blue powder burn plainly visible under his right eye. His companion was slightly shorter but stolidly built with the look of a bruiser — Fairfax and his friend who had given him such a rough handling at the Blue Duck!

Dacers supressed a chuckle. He had timed everything just about right, the pair were apparently on their way to Cardsworth by the same train as himself to keep their appointment with Sir Oswald Vaillant.

Although the two Americans passed quite close to him they never looked in his direction and, since they had encountered him only in the dark when he was garbed in a fustian suit, it was unlikely that, had they seen him, they would recognise him in brighter light and in his different clothing.

He reached the window, bought a second-class return ticket to Tringford then walked quickly towards the platforms, hoping to catch sight of the pair and follow them. He saw their twin tall hats bobbing through the crowd and he walked behind them, keeping them in view until they came to the platform where the hissing and steaming locomotive of the north bound train waited with its string of carriages whose design showed their descent from the old stage coaches, made obsolete by the railways.

Knots of passengers were struggling through the narrow doors of the carriages and, seeing the pair he shadowed enter one close to the engine, he made for one nearer the rear. A few minutes later, wheezing, snorting and chuffing, the train jerked into motion. Dacers settled down to a ride of small comfort, crammed between a fat man who looked like a farmer and a middle-aged woman whose expanse of crinoline took up more than her ticket's worth of space. Mercifully, it was a short journey to Tringford and when a porter on the platform called out the name of the station, Dacers stumbled over an assortment of feet to reach the door. He was the only passenger to depart.

Cautiously, wary of the two Americans in the carriage ahead, he stepped down to the platform of a modest country station. With a corner of his eye, he saw the two dark clad men with their stove pipe hats, alighting. Both did so without looking his way and they and Dacers were the only ones to get out of the train. The two walked off towards the end of the platform close at hand to them where there was a gate, which seemed to open up on to a road. He slipped behind a building housing a waiting room to keep out of their sight and made a business of fumbling in the pocket of his top coat as if seeking his ticket to give the two time to leave the station.

When the pair were out of sight, he took his time in walking along the platform towards the gate and recalled what he had learned of the locality from another reference in his library, a large scale map of the country within a wide range of London. The hamlet of Cardsworth was shown a short distance along a country road, a continuation of the main street of Tringford on which the railway station was situated. Just before it was reached from the station, a symbol denoted a substantial building marked *Manor House*, some distance from the road and in spacious lands. Plainly, it was Fairwinds Manor, the residence of Sir Oswald Vaillant. It was an easy walk from the station.

The station gate opened on to the sleepy looking, unpaved principal street of Tringford, obviously a market town, probably attractive in summer but uninspiring on a wintery day. Many of its cottages were old and thatched. Outside the station stood a horse and trap of the kind commonly for hire at railway stations, with a driver who looked at Dacers expectantly. Dacers shook his head, he had no intention of hiring a vehicle, knowing that his destination was within walking distance. Then, at the further end of the street, he saw another trap progressing out of town in the direction of the hamlet of Cardsworth. The tall hats of its two passengers told him that his attackers of the previous night, now looking so staid, were calling on Sir Oswald Vaillant in a style suggesting blameless respectability.

As the hired trap disappeared around a bend at the end of the street, Dacers set off walking in the same direction. The little town was soon left behind and he was walking along a broad lane with thick hawthorn hedges on its margins. Remembering the outlines of the map, he looked out for landmarks and eventually, away to his left, he saw the tall chimneys of a large house on a hill and he soon passed a set of tall iron gates over which ornately fashioned letters read: *Fairwinds Manor* and a wide gravel drive led from them in the direction of the mansion. Doubtless, the two Americans had reached the manor by now.

Dacers wanted to learn something of Sir Oswald Vaillant as much as he desired to know what business the tall-hatted pair had with him but he knew how strangers in remote, tight-knit communities attracted attention and were remembered. He would need to guard against being too persistent and asking too many questions if he had contact with any of the local people. That was if he met any. On the walk along the lane he had not encountered a single human being. Attuned to the pace of crowded, hurrying London as he was, he found the stillness and emptiness of this rural retreat almost eerie.

Then, a short way past the gates of the manor, he came upon a little cluster of small cottages, probably centuries old, obviously the hamlet of Cardsworth. More prominent was a taller building at the end of the row of dwellings: an inn with a black-and-white frontage suggesting Elizabethan origins. Its sign bore a heraldic device and the legend: *The Vaillant Arms*. So the Vaillant family were long rooted in the region and, clearly, major landowners.

A tavern was always a good place to seek local knowledge but caution would be required if he was not to make himself too conspicuous. It was close to noon and the need for sustenance gave him an excuse to enter the hostelry.

The interior had low beams of stout oak, a general air of antiquity and the welcome sight of a fire blazing in the grate. It was empty save for a plump, jovial looking man behind the bar, without question the landlord, who greeted Dacers cheerfully with an observation on the brightness of the day, even though it was cold.

'Cold but healthy enough, I think, landlord. I'll have a pint of ale, if you please, and can you provide any bread and cheese?'

The landlord beamed. 'I can, sir, and capital cheese at that, churned by my own wife.' With the inquisitiveness of a countryman encountering a stranger in his village, a kind of inquisitiveness of which Dacers was wary, he asked: 'You going far, sir, I see you're afoot.'

'Quite right. I don't run to a fancy coach like a gig or even a modest pony and trap, I fear. I'm just a toiler, tied to a desk in London nearly all year round. I have a couple of free days and decided on a stroll away from the city smoke. I was always fond of Hertfordshire but I don't know this part very well.'

'Oh, it's a pleasant place, sir. At its best in summer, of course, but, on the whole, as comfortable a spot as any.'

'Much like your own excellent premises,' Dacers said, seating himself at an oaken table near the fire.

The landlord served him with a tankard of ale, disappeared into the inner regions of the premises then emerged with a plateful of bread and cheese. He occupied a chair opposite his guest, obviously in the mood for a chat. 'I hope you don't object to my company, sir,' he said. 'Things are always slack this time of year and it's pleasant to have a visitor.'

'Not at all,' said Dacers, disguising his wariness. Then he ventured: 'I noticed a handsome looking house yonder on the hill.' He hoped he did not sound like a London criminal 'casing' the opulent looking mansion as a 'crib' to be robbed.

'You mean the Manor. That's the home

of Sir Oswald Vaillant, who's more or less our squire. The family's been here all through history and own nearly all Cardsworth.'

'Is he a good squire?' asked Dacers.

The landlord made a sour face. 'That's a matter of opinion. He's our leading magistrate and a man in my trade can't criticise magistrates too much. They have too much power over licensing. But I must say Sir Oswald is hard in the punishments he hands out. He hates the local poachers and they hate him in return. He has a foul tempered game-keeper and vicious mantraps on his land to keep poachers away. And there's other things about him that some folk ain't happy with. He has big stakes in shipping and shipbuilding and American cotton. Well, you know how them rebel states in America had raiding ships built on the sly here in England that set off and sank United States' ships all around the world?'

'Of course: the *Shenandoah* and the famous *Alabama* and many others.' Dacers felt his heart leap at this mention of the American war. Once again, this recent upheaval of a nation was coming into the picture.

'Well,' continued the landlord, 'you'll know how pots of money from our wealthy business people went into those schemes, particularly from shipbuilders, shipping firms and the cotton men up north who were starved of raw cotton because the Northern navy blockaded the Southern ports, stopping exports. It was all secret at first, but word leaked out. Sir Oswald was very much in on supplying money and shipbuilding facilities, propping up the cause of the Confederate States. That was all wrong in my opinion.'

'You're uncommonly well informed,' observed Dacers, recalling his own acquaintance with such matters and his trip to Liverpool with Theodore Van Trask but keeping his own counsel.

'Oh. I've always watched the ways of the world, always read the newspapers, even if I do live in a little place like this,' said the landlord proudly. 'I don't like to be thought an ignorant yokel. Don't get me wrong about them Southern states.

They fought bravely for what they believed in and their people suffered awful hardships. But it was slavery that I disagreed with. It couldn't be right to work people as if they were animals and to buy and sell them in the way farmers deal in cattle.' The landlord paused and gave Dacers a dubious look. Even in an England that had abolished slavery in its own territories long before, there were divided opinions on the subject. Many English families of importance owed their wealth to generations of slave trading, supplying the American plantations with captive Africans.

Septimus Dacers caught the meaning of his pause. 'Oh, I agree with you wholeheartedly, being of a radical turn of mind myself,' he said.

The landlord looked relieved. 'It's the way I was brought up, you see. My old father was a Chartist and I took after him. You know how the People's Charter called for a fairer deal all round for ordinary people. It's a great pity the Chartist movement failed.'

On finishing his refreshment, Dacers

thanked the landlord for his hospitality, praised the excellent quality of his wife's cheese then departed the Vaillant Arms, hoping that the landlord did not notice that he followed the route that brought him to the hostelry: in short, he was returning to Fairwinds Manor highly grateful for the intelligence his host at the tavern had imparted.

He reached the manor just as the early gloom of a winter's day set in. Again, the laneway outside the gates was quiet and minus any sign of pedestrians or vehicles. Having come this far, he wanted his trip into the country to yield something fruitful and he thought of prowling around the house to try to catch some knowledge of what went on between the local squire and his American visitors. The thought of bone-crunching mantraps and a fierce gamekeeper and, doubtless, one or more dogs, caused him to pause but they were surely hazards to be encountered in the manor's surrounding, poachable agricultural lands. He could see through the bars of the great metal gates that the wide drive led through a spacious, well cultivated garden where any such dangers would be unlikely.

Just as he was wondering about his chances of entering the manor's grounds, he heard the smart tramp of hoofs and the rumble of wheels approaching from the direction of the town. Instinctively, he dived into the dry ditch alongside the blackthorn hedge very close to the gates. He crouched in the ditch, trying to make himself as small as possible.

Peering gingerly over the verge of the ditch, he saw a horse and trap, probably one of those available to passengers arriving at the railway station, coming along the lane. It contained one top-hatted passenger, whose style echoed that of the two already at the manor.

Sure enough, as the vehicle drew nearer, Dacers recognised the driver who had looked at him, hopeful for his patronage, when he arrived at the station. So a third visitor had arrived by train and was bound for Fairwinds Manor, it seemed.

He crouched lower in the ditch as the vehicle drew nearer and, just before he did so, the trap drew near enough for him to have a fuller if fleeting view of the passenger. He was a small man with a distinct hump on his back. Could this be the Fortune of whom he had heard mention? And, surely, he was the hunchback whom Roberta Van Trask glimpsed as the carriage sped away from outside her home.

The vehicle halted at the gates of the manor and the driver left his seat, walked to the gates and drew back a bolt then shoved the heavy gate open. The operation surprised Dacers, he had expected a servant to appear from somewhere and attend to that chore. So now he knew the gates could be operated from the outside. The trap was now near enough to the ditch for Dacers to see that the hunchback had a large black box on his knee.

The driver returned to his seat and urged the horse forward and the trap rolled through the gates. It stopped again, the driver descended and closed the gates. Dacers waited until the sound of the wheels on the driveway died away then came out of the ditch.

Several sentiments burned in him now. He desired revenge for his humiliation the night before; he had a sharpened curiosity about the three now gathered at Sir Oswald Vaillant's home, what they were up to and where they fitted into the affairs of Theodore Van Trask. Also, though he would be loath to admit it, he had an almost boyish wish to play the knight in shining armour for the charming and spirited Miss Roberta Van Trask.

The exertions of his walk plus his crouching in the ditch brought some twinges of pain from the knife wound in his side but, gripped by his detective's determination, he decided on a bold excursion into the domain of the squire of Cardsworth, hoping he did not encounter the foul tempered gamekeeper the landlord of the hostelry had mentioned.

The gloom of a rapidly closing day had intensified as he operated the bolt of the gate, swung it open and stepped on to the path. He surveyed the wide sweep of the garden before him. It slanted upward towards the house on the hill, separated from him by an expanse of carefully tended lawn, with various ornamental shrubs and statuary placed at intervals. Dacers gave a grunt of satisfaction as he studied the prospect like a military man assessing terrain he was about to cross.

The gathering gloom would offer some cover and, if he kept low and dodged behind the shrubs and statues, he might not be spotted from the house.

He bent low and moved fast, heading at a run for a neatly trimmed bush standing a few yards away. He scuttled behind it and recovered his breath, wincing a little at the pain in his side. He made another dash for the cover of a Roman style statue of a man in a toga, then a longer run to finish behind another bush. Now he was close to the top of the rise on which the manor house stood and he could see that all its windows were heavily curtained.

Another couple of swift dashes brought him within yards of the manor and he hoped that no servants were out of doors in its vicinity and, particularly, that there were no dogs to raise an alarm. He was close to a broad ground floor window and could hear a buzz of conversation coming from behind it. The window was curtained like the others but a chink of subdued yellow light escaped from a point near the bottom of the pane where two of the drapes had not been fully drawn together.

He crept forward, went on his knees on a flowerbed underneath the window and looked through the small gap in the curtains.

He saw only a portion of what was going on in the room but it was a revealing picture. There were four men: a pot bellied individual with a full beard and a hawk nose, doubtless Sir Oswald Vaillant. Next to him were two men of whom he could see only a portion but they must have been the pair he clashed with at the Blue Duck while the little hunchback was clearly visible.

He was standing behind a table, which bore a device he was operating, very likely the contents of the black box he brought with him. It was a recently introduced novelty called a 'magic lantern' and the reason for the subdued lighting in the room because the man — whom he believed to be Fortune — was projecting a picture on to a white sheet.

The projected image, of which Dacers could see only a part, was of some kind of engineering drawing, seeming to be the plan of an extremely narrow boat, with notes and symbols lettered along the margins.

The squire of Cardsworth and the smaller man were talking earnestly but Dacers could not catch their words. Then, he chanced to see several horizontal slots drilled into a brick just below the heavy windowsill. It was a ventilation brick, which allowed some air into the room.

Bending yet lower, Dacers put his ear to the brick and he heard the voice of Sir Oswald quite distinctly. He was gruff and had the loud, hectoring delivery of the English upper classes when dealing with those they considered their inferiors:

' . . . but, dammit, Fortune, the *Hunley* was a total failure,' he was saying. 'She sank three times as I remember, each time with the loss of her crew, including her inventor, Hunley himself, in the second disaster. I can't see anyone risking money on such a project. It would be folly.'

'Yes, she sank, Sir Oswald, because she was not fully developed. She was hastily created under the pressures of the war. And, with respect, I beg to differ. She was not a total failure,' Fortune responded in a subservient tone. 'Before she finally went down, she proved her worth by sinking a United States' vessel many times her size, the *Housetanic*, which was blockading the South Carolina coast. But that was the old, experimental *Hunley*. These plans of ours are for a much improved — indeed, a totally perfected — version of such a craft. Her ballast tanks, air chambers and crew's quarters are designed to the most modern and scientific standards and she will be perfectly safe. She cannot fail. All we need is the money to develop her and other untried but ingenious inventions for the good of a revitalised South, which will be victorious. A whole nation is waiting only to be fully armed to plunge into a war of revenge. Whatever you put in will be a sound investment.'

'Really?' came Vaillant's hooting tones. 'Bound to bring a good return if a fellow backs it, what? An absolutely sound proposition is it?' The knight's voice fairly dripped greed.

'Completely sound, Sir Oswald,' said Fortune. 'Every bit as sound as the determination of the Resurgent South, as we have named ourselves or, if you like, The Dixie Ghosts — the revitalised spirits of the Confederacy, returned to wreak vengeance on the Yankee conquerors, seek justice and re-establish the old Southern order of life. You may be sure all donors to our cause will be richly rewarded after our victory.'

Septimus Dacers gave a low whistle of surprise and his mind began to race. Who hadn't heard of the *Hunley* during the American Civil War? She was something new in naval warfare, an undersea boat. What was the term for her? A *submarine!* She represented highly imaginative naval engineering — but she was tragically ill-fated.

And there was Fortune's talk of he and

his henchmen and a body of unknown strength as the Resurgent South or The Dixie Ghosts! Could there really be enough fit manpower in the South straining at the leash to rally to a call to fight anew with improved weaponry, paid for by their wealthy capitalist friends in the United Kingdom? Could they really vanquish the powerful Northern states and re-establish the old Southern order with a return to the discredited institution that underpinned it — slavery? It seemed unlikely but it was a stunning prospect and nothing less was being promoted by the three Americans. Dacers gave another low whistle and clapped his ear to the ventilation brick again.

4

Journey in the Fog

Dacers, still crouching in the flowerbed under the window, heard a buzz of mingled conversations and bodily movements as if the magic lantern show was concluded and the meeting was breaking up. He rose slightly and looked through the limited aperture again, seeing the occupants of the room moving around and he had a clear view of Fortune packing the magic lantern into the black box.

The conversation he had just heard set questions whirling through his head. How could Sir Oswald Vaillant's visitors even think of re-igniting the war in America when the South had been beaten into utter exhaustion? And where did Theodore Van Trask fit into this puzzle? Was this outlandish scheme the 'something' his daughter felt her father was entangled in? But Van Trask was a stolidly loyal citizen of the United States who had served his country with distinction for years. And there was the further riddle of why he was attacked out of the blue by one of the plotters, the pistol wielding ruffian calling himself Fairfax.

He was jerked out of his speculation by the sound of voices from one side of the house and he realised that the main entrance to the manor was at that side and the visitors were leaving by it. Then came the rumble of wheels and the clop of a horse. He had not realised that the station trap that brought Fortune had waited, probably in a stable yard at the rear of the house.

Dacers flattened himself against the winter damp soil of the flower bed and held his breath. He was thankful that it was now almost dark. Also a slight fog was descending and he was some distance from the driveway. The trap containing the tall-hatted silhouettes of the three passed near enough to him for him to hear the voice of the hunchback, Fortune, harsh, testy and loud. He was plainly angry enough not to care that the driver of the hired vehicle could hear what he was saying.

'At least you managed to keep your mouth shut in there, Cal Tebbutt. I don't know what the Yankees hit you with in the battle of Shiloh, but it sure loosened your tongue and made your behaviour all fired erratic. In future, say nothing and don't fly off the handle. That damn fool performance with old Van Trask could have delivered a mule kick to our plans if Adams and his crew got word of it. In future, keep dumb, like Meakum, here.'

Dacers remembered from the attack at the Blue Duck that 'Cal' was the one who called himself Fairfax but his real name was Tebbutt and he had displayed a tendency towards impetuous, near hysterical outbursts. Once again, he felt the cold mouth of the Derringer against his temple and heard the quivering, edgy voice threatening to blow his brains out. He sounded as if he would do just that only for the cautioning of his accomplice, apparently named Meakum.

His eavesdropping under the window

had revealed the important fact that Fortune was certainly the leading figure of the group and he had been located elsewhere but now appeared to be returning to London with Fairfax and Meakum.

The vehicle disappeared into what was now thickening fog and Dacers remained lying on the ground until he heard the closing clang of the great gate to the estate. Then he rose and hastened out of the garden before anyone from the house chanced to make an appearance.

Out in the lane, there was every indication that the fog was becoming denser and it was likely that the whole countryside would soon be under a dense blanket. He had yet to return to Tringford to take the train back to London but, since it was merely a straight walk along the lane, he could not become lost so long as he kept to the lane. If he blundered into the hedges and ditches on either side of the track he would know he was wandering off course.

He reasoned that the three Americans would catch a train before him and it would suit him to take a later one. He had no desire to encounter them at the railway station. His running and crouching had awakened some of the pain in his injured side and he hoped the fairly long walk would not prove troublesome.

Walking steadily, he progressed along the unpaved and rutted lane blanketed by the swirling greyness of the fog, which would probably last all night. Typical of a man in a fog, he tended to occasionally wander to one side or the other without meaning to, but he always found the centre of the lane again.

He reached the principal street of Tringford, finding that the town had no gaslights, only dim oil lamps placed at intervals. At the station, however, there was more light, some of it moving about as several railway employees were swinging lanterns on the 'up' platform for London. Like grey spectres, there were a number of men on the platform shifting about restlessly and the huge bulk of a locomotive with a string of carriages stood against the platform. The firebox of the engine gave out a vivid crimson and yellow illumination to add to the eeriness of the scene.

Only a few of the waiting passengers were from Tringford. Many of the others had boarded the train at distant stations further north but, in spite of the fog, they had stepped out on to the platform to smoke during the delay. For the male of the species, the bane of railway travel was the constant complaining of the ladies when men dared to light their cigars or pipes in the cramped confines of the carriages.

A man in a gold braided frock coat and tall hat, obviously the stationmaster, was standing at the gate as Dacers entered the station.

'D'you want this train, sir?' he asked. 'Kindly make haste. She's ready to move. She came in more than an hour late due to dense fog further north and she's been further delayed here. Jump aboard, sir, we want to get her on her way.'

Along the platform the lantern carrying porters were herding the ghostly and mostly disgruntled passengers towards the carriages. As they did so, a ray of lantern light struck the face of one of the men not far from Dacers and just as it did so, he turned his head and looked directly at Dacers. With a chill running through his body, Dacers found that he was looking at the fair moustached face of Fairfax, otherwise Tebbutt. The American's eyes widened. There was absolutely no doubt that he recognised Dacers and violent hostility showed in the lamplit visage.

The porter swung his lantern, putting Fairfax back under the blanketing fog, and he shouted: 'Take your seats, please, gentlemen. The train's moving in a minute.' He and his colleagues shooed the passengers into the coaches and Dacers dived into the nearest one.

So the trio of Americans had not gone ahead of him thanks to the delaying fog and, again, he was travelling with them on the same train. They would certainly be intrigued by his presence in the region where they had kept their appointment with Sir Oswald Vaillant. Could he expect trouble if he encountered them at Euston?

The great locomotive started its puffing and grunting and added to the density of the fog by belching gouts of black smoke out of its huge funnel. The carriages jerked and, cautiously, the train moved forward into the enveloping murkiness.

It made slow progress, stopping several times between stations because more lantern wielding men on the tracks gave warnings of danger at points and junctions and it was nearly midnight when it finally steamed into Euston Station. Septimus Dacers, sharing a seat with two scarlet-coated soldiers, a woman with a pair of unruly small boys and a corpulent clergyman who managed to sleep all the way, despite the noise of the two youngsters, found the journey an annoying ordeal. Throughout it, his mind was on the three exiles from Dixie and whether they would force a clash with him at Euston.

When they arrived, the trainload of passengers spilled out and began to move along the platform in a weary herd. In the jostle of tall hats and bonnets, Dacers could not identify the three Americans but knew they must be somewhere in the throng. He was certain that there would be some reaction from them after spotting him at Tringford — and it was likely to be unpleasant. He had the uneasy thought that they might have positioned themselves behind him and were following him — or had they gone ahead, intending to waylay him?

A form of lethargy took hold of him. He was stiff and weary and the knife wound Dandy Jem had given him still caused twinges of pain. After the strenuous day, his thoughts turned to the comfortable bed waiting at his lodgings.

In the station's great hall, the flow from the Tringford train merged with a sea of passengers from those arrived from various parts of the country, all delayed by the fog. Forcing himself into alertness, he looked around the multitude but still saw nothing of the American trio.

Outside, there was a regular 'pea souper' of a London fog more usual in November than February and fractious passengers began to squabble over hiring hansom cabs from the line waiting along

Drummond Street in front of the station. Dacers was grateful that his home base was within walking distance and he set off, plodding on heavy feet.

The route was familiar but he had to pick his way through the smother relying on various familiar landmarks as they loomed into view. Nearing home, what he heard at Cardsworth forced itself upon his consciousness. Could a mere three men really restart the American Civil war, or were they part of a larger conspiracy? How could the economy of the South be restored when the foundation of the old agricultural order was slavery, now totally discredited by all the civilised world? Had the conspirators really redesigned the *Hunley*, the experimental underwater boat with a tragic history, and made it in to a viable vessel of war?

Through a combination of deep thought, fatigue and caution in the unfavourable weather conditions, Dacers failed to notice that, every step of the way, he was followed by a man of small stature who kept a few paces behind, veiled by swirls of sulphurous fog. He walked with the silence of a cat. He was a lantern jawed man with glittering eyes and a humped back.

He reached the square where his lodgings were located, entered it thankfully and reached the darkened house where Mrs. Slingsby and Emma, the maid of all work, would have long been asleep. He mounted the steps with his key in his hand and silently opened the street door. Fortune, the man who had trailed him, stood back, out of view in the fog and when the door closed on Dacers, he stepped forward, stopped at the bottom of the steps to ascertain the number of the house then left the square. His bushy brows were drawn over his eyes and his mouth was set in a grimly determined line.

In the entrance hall of the house, Septimus Dacers turned up the illumination of the gaslight, which was kept at a low level throughout the night. He saw that a silver plate lay on a small table and on it was a letter addressed in a neat and attractive hand to: '*S. Dacers Esq.*'

He opened the pleasantly perfumed

envelope. In the same neat hand was the message:

'Dear Mr Dacers.

If it is convenient, could you kindly meet me in the Tea Room of Carrington's Hotel, St James's Place, at 11 a.m. tomorrow?

Roberta Van Trask.'

5

The Vanishing Hump

'You found your letter, Mr. Dacers? It was delivered by a messenger boy yesterday,' said Mrs. Slingsby as Dacers was breakfasting next morning.

'Yes, thank you, Mrs Slingsby.'

His landlady nodded and gave him a knowing smile as if they shared a secret. She had obviously noted the perfumed stationery and while she did not want to lose her lodger for all his unorthodox comings and goings and his often hazardous lifestyle, she hoped that when she did, it would be to a 'nice wife'. She greatly hoped that the charming American girl who had called a short time before had a significance in Dacers' life.

Dacers finished his breakfast and readied himself to keep his appointment with Miss Van Trask and stepped out into a London cityscape now largely cleared of fog.

Carrington's Hotel was an elegant establishment frequented by the well heeled and it presented its well-bred frontage to equally well-bred and fashionable St James's Place.

A little before 11 a.m. Dacers, fitted out to appear in such an environment in a slate grey frock coat, a well brushed tall hat and carrying a stick, climbed the hotel's broad steps and entered, acknowledging the salute of the doorman who was garbed in a silver frogged coat of military scarlet, velvet knee breeches and a powdered wig.

He found the Tea Room to be a tranquil place, thickly carpeted and cluttered with potted ferns while its walls were overburdened with paintings in gilded frames. Tea drinkers sat at ornate tables between which waiters glided silently as if on well-oiled castors.

Roberta Van Trask was sitting at a corner table accompanied by a young black woman in a winter outfit of bonnet and crinoline as fashionable and tasteful as those of Miss Van Trask herself. Dacers approached them, raising his hat and Roberta Van Trask gave him her warm and modest smile.

'So good of you to come at such short notice, Mr. Dacers,' she said. 'This is Esther, my maid. She is perfectly discreet and we can talk quite freely in her presence. She is my friend as well as my maid. I want to keep our meeting rather secret because I do not wish my father to have word of my trying to get to the bottom of whatever is troubling him so much. He thinks Esther and I are on a shopping trip. Tell me, are you any further on with your investigations?'

Dacers sat down on a vacant chair and balanced his tall hat on his knee. 'Let's say I have had some contact with certain people from over the ocean and they have something afoot, but I have yet to unravel where their activities fit into Mr Van Trask's affairs, if indeed they do. With your permission, I'll tell you in fuller detail when I know more. Please do not worry yourself. I am doing my very best to help you. I'm sure things will come to a good conclusion.'

He hoped that last sentiment would not prove false and felt that, for the present, he was unable to tell her anything about a scheme so outlandish as reviving a belligerent Southern Confederacy in case she worried that her father was in some way implicated in the plot.

He needed to know more and did not yet know what his next move would be. It was his fervent hope that it would not reveal that Theodore Van Trask was entangled in the scheming of Messrs Fortune, Fairfax and Meakum and whoever else might be involved.

'I'm content to allow you to do as you think fit, Mr. Dacers,' said the girl. 'I wanted, however, to tell you something that might be useful. You will recall that I told you I felt I had seen the man I believed to be a hunchback before. The one I glimpsed in the carriage on the day that man Fairfax attacked my father — well, I've remembered where I saw him.'

'Really? Where?

'In Willard's Hotel in Washington.

Willard's is a kind of crossroads. In the war, everybody of note and some dubious people lived or met there: politicians, officers of the army and navy; newspapermen; contractors looking for government business and mysterious men and women possibly spying for one side or the other. Virginia, in enemy territory, lay on the other side of the Potomac River and, in spite of all the precautions of both sides, secret agents from both the Union and the Confederacy managed to cross the river quite frequently. Willard's Hotel was always a hotbed of rumour and dubious goings-on. And that's where I saw the man, deep in conversation with Colonel Baker.'

'Who's Colonel Baker?' Dacers asked.

'Colonel Lafayette Baker was one of the most powerful and intriguing men in Washington and there were always whispers about him,' said Miss Van Trask. 'Some suggested he was not wholly loyal to the Union and there were ugly rumours about his past. Before the war, he was said to have been a leader of the San Francisco Vigilantes, who pursued suspected criminals and even hanged them from lampposts without trial. During the war, he headed the National Detective Police Force, which he founded and, in fact, he was the Union's spymaster. More recently, further rumours have been flying because he posted a man at the box in Ford's Theatre to guard President and Mrs. Lincoln but he deserted his post, allowing John Wilkes Booth to enter and shoot Mr. Lincoln. It seems Colonel Baker never punished the policeman. I hear this is much talked of with suspicion in Washington.'

'That is indeed interesting, Miss Van Trask,' commented Dacers.

'And something very puzzling, Mr. Dacers is that I am absolutely certain that, when I saw the man with Colonel Baker, he did not have a hunched back. He was completely free of any deformity. Here in London, I only glimpsed the man in the carriage as it sped off, of course, but I'm sure he was a hunchback.'

'Possibly, you were mistaken and they were two different men.'

'No, there was something quite unforgettable about that lean face, those heavy eyebrows and those glittering eyes. I remember them so well and, just yesterday, I suddenly recalled the scene in Willard's Hotel, during the war between the states.'

'Well,' ventured Dacers 'There might have been two men — identical twins, one of whom was unfortunate enough to have a spinal abnormality.'

The girl shook her head. 'I thought of that but, somehow, it doesn't ring true. I'm somehow sure he was one and the same man. You can call it a woman's intuition if you like.'

Dacers went a jump ahead of her. 'So, you're thinking if this man was so clearly one of those associated with the Fairfax fellow, who was definitely from the rebel South, why was he hobnobbing with the Union's spymaster during the war?'

Dacers determined that, for the present, he would keep her in the dark about his knowing Fortune's name as well as having some knowledge of his activities on this side of the Atlantic until he had a fuller picture of the plot Fortune, Fairfax and Meakum were attempting to further. Her revelation of his meeting with Colonel Lafayette Baker might throw some light on his character, if she had not mistaken the identity of the man at Willard's Hotel.

'Could it be,' he asked, 'that the man was playing a double game — spying for both sides; working for Baker on the Union side and for the Confederacy as well? But who can say where his true allegiance lay?'

'Exactly and there *were* double agents,' she said. 'But what about that hump? How is it that a man is a hunchback when seen in England, but not when seen in America?'

Dacers shrugged. 'Who can say? Unless, and I hesitate to suggest it again, you were mistaken, Miss Van Trask'.

But, much earlier in their conversation, he had begun to form an answer to that question, but that was something else he decided to keep to himself for the present.

'Well, for whatever it is worth, I thought I should tell you about it,' said the girl. 'I may be prejudiced but I suppose my long residence in Washington has made me feel that any connection with Colonel Baker makes a thing that much more sinister.' She paused and looked at Dacers squarely, curious about bruises from the Blue Duck episode on his face.

She frowned and asked: 'Mr. Dacers, do I see marks of injury on your face? I do hope your efforts on my behalf have not led you into physical danger.'

Dacers surprised himself by his own out-of-character boldness by replying: 'If they did, Miss Van Trask, what are a few bruises if they are earned in the service of a lady?'

Esther, the maid and companion, placed her hand to her mouth to suppress a giggle and Roberta Van Trask gave a silvery peal of laughter, which was a delight to hear since she was previously so burdened with care. Then she said demurely: 'Why, Mr. Dacers, what a perfect Englishman you are! Such chivalry!'

Septimus Dacers left Carrington's

Hotel with his thoughts on the man who might or might not have a hump on his back but overriding them was the echo of Roberta Van Trask's attractive laughter.

And it brought an unaccustomed lightness of heart and a matching lightness of step.

Elsewhere and a little earlier, the activities of Messrs Fortune, Fairfax and Meakum had begun to have an effect.

Shortly before Miss Van Trask called on Septimus Dacers in London, a certain Sheffield ironmaster, in his office in the midst of his smoke choked furnaces and forges, opened a letter addressed to him, marked 'Strictly Private'.

It consisted of two sheets of flowery but highly tempting prose under a strikingly engraved heading which embodied the St. Andrew's cross studded with stars, called 'the Stars and Bars', the standard of the now defunct Confederate States of America, which, in 1861, launched the bloody civil war. As the ironmaster read it, his usually dour face brightened and his eyes became enlivened.

During the war in America, he helped

to finance the building of some of the secret sea craft created for the Confederates in British yards to raid and sink U.S. shipping and break the United States' blockade of the Southern coast and bring out exports, chiefly of the South's most important commodity, raw cotton. He had also invested heavily in shares in other such enterprises. The financial returns were good and, of course, the ironmaster could make the humane excuse that it was all done to help the workers in the cotton mills of northern England who were on the edge of starvation due to the 'Cotton Famine' brought about by the United States' blockade.

He never heeded the fact that the working men of Manchester had addressed a letter to Lincoln, applauding his anti-slavery sentiments and saying they preferred hardship to handling cotton made available through the inhuman use of black slaves. Nor, for all his professed charitable concern for the cotton workers of Lancashire, did he consider taking any action to ease the sweated conditions in his own workshops which were little better than those endured by the transatlantic slaves.

The letter, headed by an engraved depiction of the Confederate flag, surrounded by warlike implements, promised a return to the good times. It opened possibilities for making more money. For it trumpeted the message that the Confederate States were not crushed. A combination of devoted men was working to revive the Southern cause. The letter said they were properly called The Resurgent South but they thought of themselves as 'The Dixie Ghosts', out to wreak revenge on the Union. Once more, under their inspiration, Southern men would throng to the beloved but conquered banner, eager to fight to create a new and powerful independent Dixie.

It would require finances, of course, but the promoters of the New South, aided by prominent Confederate citizens and former officers of the Southern army and navy and a wealth of others devoted to the gallant South, confidently expected their old supporters to rally to their aid, unstinting as before.

For the South would fight again and being now equipped with many advanced devices and inventions of war developed in secret with Southern ingenuity but not released in the war, triumph over Dixie's enemies was assured.

There was much more stirring prose, which made a powerful appeal to the ironmaster's strongly developed appreciation of profit.

Then there was the owner of mines in the Lancashire coalfields who received the same letter. Twice, before the British government stopped the use of young children and women in mines, his company had been castigated by official inquiries for their inhuman usage and his ignoring of even such feeble measures as then protected these vulnerable toilers. Such a man might be expected to support a cause that had slavery as a main plank of its constitution. And he did, giving generous aid to create the secretly built sea craft. Now the high-flown appeal for funds awoke memories of the profits made from his shares in the enterprises that supplied arms and shipping to the rebel states. He began to consider loosening his purse strings yet again.

A retired British Army general in Dorset; a crusty old judge in Berkshire; a one time high ranking civil servant in London and a reclusive old resident of Birmingham, reputed to be a miser, all of whom had invested in shares in the British firms involved in providing warlike supplies and shipping for the Confederacy also received the letter, which quickened their hearts when they read it.

Such was the appeal to avarice made by the letter that its recipients did not pause to consider the true condition of the Southern states since the surrender of their armies and the fall of their capital, Richmond, Virginia. For the cream of Dixie's fighting young manhood was dead or crippled; life giving crops were ruined by marauding Northern forces; poverty and hunger stalked the scene of the defeated South which the triumphant Union was trying to remake under its policy of 'Reconstruction.'

The letter was also received by a solidly built, middle-aged man with a bald head and luxurious muttonchop whiskers in his lodgings in the Toxteth district of Liverpool. In his case, it was sent not by its originators but by a person who enclosed a covering note:

'*Commander Bulloch, Sir,*

This letter is going the rounds of certain gentlemen who are mostly known to yourself and who aided your activities of an earlier date. I think you will agree that it is a barefaced and audacious attempt at a confidence trick. Perhaps you feel that the recipients should be protected from the designs on their funds, which the organisers of the scheme so obviously entertain. You may be inclined to take some action to preserve the good name of decent Southern people, although I know that your present situation means you are severely restricted in what you can do. I, too, am extremely restricted but I see this scheme as a disgraceful use of the plight of a defeated, grieving but gallant people for tawdry gain. The promoters are certainly criminals.

'You know me, sir, but I prefer to sign myself, simply
    A Friend in London.'

James Bulloch, sometime an officer of the United States' Navy and more recently a commander in the Confederate States' Navy, having followed his native Georgia in the revolt against Lincoln's government, stared at the accompanying letter for a few seconds then gave a bark of laughter which contained no hint of humour. He turned to the tall, slim younger man with a black moustache sitting across the room.

'Irvine,' he called. 'You have to read this. When it comes to confidence trickery it beats all those tales of sharp Yankees selling gold bricks or all Broadway to yokels for a couple of dollars.'

The younger man, Irvine Bulloch, ex-lieutenant of the Confederate Navy and the half brother of the commander was the sailing master of the celebrated *Shenandoah*, who had navigated that celebrated raider on her last epic voyage to Liverpool. He took the missive, studied its bellicose illustrated heading then read it with widening eyes. 'High falutin' sentiments, Jim,' he commented. 'And there is even a claim that the promoters are in possession of the missing Great Seal of the Confederacy as well as important government documents'. He began to quote:

'We would point out that interest has been shown in our newly developed weapons by a revolutionary brother-hood, backed by strong Irish-American interests and sworn enemies of Queen Victoria and her government. We need hardly tell you that no patriotic Englishman would wish to see them fall into such hands.'

'Outright blackmail!' exclaimed Irvine. 'They are suggesting they would sell these imaginary weapons to the Irish Fenians if money is not raised from British sources.'
He continued to read:

'To fortify their claim to act in the spirit of the old Confederate States, the

promoters give an assurance that they hold the Great Seal of the Confederacy, believed to be lost since the fall of Richmond. This solid silver work of art is as sacred as the ancient Great Seal of Great Britain and whoever owns it can claim absolutely to have the right and duty to administer and protect the constitution of the Confederate States as drawn up and administered by the founding fathers and to claim the adherence and loyalty of all citizens of those states.'

Irvine Bulloch frowned. 'Why, that's a damned lie, Jim!' he exploded. 'The Great Seal disappeared since the war ended. We've all heard the rumour that the Yankees seized it and melted it down for the silver. These scoundrels can't possibly have it!'

'It's a lie, all right,' affirmed his half brother. 'I didn't tell you before but when I sneaked off to London a few weeks ago to see some exiles from Dixie I made the acquaintance of a Mr. William Bromwell, an impoverished but loyal Southerner and a former official of our State Department in Richmond. The Great Seal was not seized by the Yankees for before Richmond fell, Bromwell secured many state papers and the Great Seal and hid them in a most secret place. He alone knows where they are and nothing will induce him to say where but he promises to do so when the time is ripe. I'm convinced it was he who sent this letter. He is one of a very small select few who know our address.' Bulloch paused and scratched his bald pate then said thoughtfully: 'I think, Irvine, in view of this piece of impudence, we shall soon have to come out of hiding and act if we have any concern for the reputation of our cause and the honour of all those who died for it. I guess we'll have to take the train for London to consult some friends of ours.'

The bald pate of James Bulloch contained many secrets, a great deal of wisdom and a wealth of cunning to the effectiveness of which Charles Francis Adams, U.S. Ambassador to the Court of St. James, could attest.

For the senior Bulloch had been the

Confederacy's chief undercover agent in Great Britain during the Civil War. It was he who raised funds for and organised the creation in Britain of ships to attack the vessels of Lincoln's navy.

Jefferson Davis, President of the Confederate States, had entrusted him with handling large sums of money, every cent of which he had carefully accounted for.

Thanks to Bulloch the rebel states acquired 'rams', used to batter in the hulls of blockading ships. There was the clipper *Sea King*, which Bulloch acquired and, in Liverpool, converted into the raider *Shenandoah*, the vessel in the news the previous year for making her way back to Liverpool six months after the war, still defiantly flying the rebel flag of Dixie.

And there was his masterpiece, the *Alabama*, created in secret in the Laird yards at Birkenhead to eventually sail all seven seas, sinking and capturing U.S. ships and earning a fearsome reputation. Her end came in the English Channel in 1864 when she clashed with the *USS Kearsarge*, which had trailed her into European waters. The *Alabama* was sunk in a tremendous battle off Cherbourg.

The always elusive Bulloch led Charles Francis Adams and his hired detectives a merry dance and it was in connection with the hunt for Bulloch and his associates that Adams sent Theodore Van Trask on his mission to Liverpool with Septimus Dacers as his bodyguard.

But the war's end brought dire hazards for James Bulloch and his half brother who, before his service in the *Shenandoah*, was the youngest officer aboard the *Alabama*, rescued after her sinking. Their wartime activities caused them to be branded pirates by the U.S. government and a return to America inevitably meant capture, trial and, almost certainly, execution for both if convicted. Although James Bulloch and his younger half brother were seen as heroes of the most courageous kind by the people of the South, the spirit of vengeance ran high among the victorious Northerners, so they lay low in Liverpool.

Each was dogged, fighting sailor and neither was a man to waste away in idleness. When word of the Resurgent South

— otherwise The Dixie Ghosts — caused the senior Bulloch to scratch his hairless head, the junior Bulloch knew something decisive would surely spring from it.

6

The Watcher in the Square

Old Dr. Alexander McLeish studied the long scar in Dacer's side from which he had just removed the tightly wound dressing and strapping. 'Aye, it's healed well,' he rumbled in his rich Scottish accent. 'Mind, you'll no doubt continue to get a twinge or two for a wee while yet and you'll carry that bonny scar to your grave. No harm in that. A few scars suggest a man's lived an eventful life, as I'll wager you have in the peculiar business you follow, Mr. Dacers. Now you're free of the bandaging, don't do any more business with villains who carry knives. You can expect my bill in the post.'

Septimus Dacers stepped out of his doctor's premises in Old Holborn and set off to thread his way through a skein of streets that would take him to Seven Dials and Setty Wilkins.

'The Dials' took its name from the junction of seven straggling mean streets and a pillar bearing seven sundials that, long ago, stood at the point of their meeting. It was a squalid, ramshackle, unhealthy and dangerous district where disease and crime stalked a maze of decaying streets. Police went into The Dials in groups and never singly. A respectably dressed stranger might lose his watch, his money or even his whole suit of clothes in an encounter with denizens of The Dials.

Grubby men with hair cropped Newgate style, and slatternly women glowered at Dacers from darkened doorways; a baby wailed somewhere; a man and woman were holding a furious, bellowing and screeching argument behind a broken window and he was approached by two small ragged boys, pleading: 'Give us a penny, guv'nor,' He ignored them, not through hard-heartedness, but if he parted with a coin, a tribe of begging youngsters would emerge from nowhere and swarm around him.

Dacers, who had ventured into many a

sector of London's murky underbelly without fear, felt as uneasy as any man every time he visited Seven Dials but Setty Wilkins was happy to dwell there for his own reasons and Dacers wished to consult him this day after his meeting with Roberta Van Trask.

He negotiated the cracked paving and broken cobbles and avoided a dead cat in his path to reach Setty's ancient dwelling-cum-workshop. He still had half a suspicion that Setty, as the only person who knew he had gone to the Blue Duck was behind his beating. But he was ashamed of it when he thought of the sterling character he knew to lie under the old engraver's eccentric front.

He entered the slanted door of the workshop and found Setty sitting on an old wooden box, smoking a clay pipe and reading a 'penny dreadful', one of the cheap sensational publications, devoured by young boys and against which clergymen preached and magistrates railed, alleging their influence was corrupting the morals of the young.

'Vy, it's Mr. Dacers again!' he exclaimed

heartily. 'You're alvays as velcome as the flowers in May, my good sir.'

Dacers nodded towards the printed paper in Setty's hand. 'Small wonder the jails are full when such fare as that is in circulation,' he said gravely.

'Come, now. If there vasn't no criminals, there vouldn't be no private inquiry agents makin' their fortunes,' Setty replied. 'Bedsides. I done the cuts in this.' He held up the paper to show a full page illustration of a terrified man being hanged in chains by a leering group of ruffians festooned with swords and pistols while a flock of wild eyed, expectant vultures flapped their wings overhead. It was headed: '*Revenge of the Highwayman's Henchmen!*' The typeface was fuzzy but Setty's handiwork as engraver of the picture was competent, sharp and clear.

'And, if no private enquiry agents, perhaps no downy birds to send them to low boozing dens to be beaten up,' rejoined Dacers, indicating the bruises on his face.

'My eye, Mr Dacers!' exclaimed Setty.

'Did that happen at the Blue Duck? I'm sorry to see it but I did give you the office that it's an uncommon rough shop.'

Dacers gave a wry grin. 'You know more than that, Setty. I never knew a man with more in his head than you. I'll wager you know a good deal more about these Americans who're to be found at the Blue Duck.'

'Vell, you only asked me if I knew vhere these Yankees congregate and I told you there's some to be found at the Blue Duck and you told me they're not likely to be Yankees but the blokes what fought the Yankees. Now, I keeps business matters confidential as a rule but I reckon I can tell you that they did a bit of business with me. Some engraving, a letterhead it seems, I'll show you a proof.'

He rose from the box, moved to a chipped and scarred oaken table, which held his proofing press and, from a drawer, produced a sheet of paper and handed it to Dacers. It bore a line illustration of a Confederate flag and the legend '*The Resurgent South*' the style suggesting the letterhead of a business concern. Dacers almost jumped when he saw that the design embodied an address for the enterprise: *'5 Blindman's Yard, Hungerford Bridge, London, England.'*

So, the men who appeared to be plotting a new civil war in America had a name for their venture and what looked like a business address quite close to the Blue Duck.

'An address in Blindman's Yard,' mused Dacers aloud. 'I believe I'll pay a call there, Setty. I wish you'd told me of it earlier.'

Setty blew out pipe smoke and stated stiffly: 'There's such a thing as confidentiality between supplier and customer, Mr. Dacers, an' I'm a business concern vot honours the proper formalities.'

Dacers studied the engraved design with intense interest. As well as the Stars and Bars of the South, there were cannon, stacked cannonballs, crossed muskets and a Latin motto of ominous significance: *Sic Semper Tyrannis* — Thus to all Tyrants. It was the motto of the State of Virginia and the cry of the Virginian John Wilkes Booth as he leapt from the theatre box having shot

Abraham Lincoln.

The whole grandiose pictorial panoply trumpeted warfare and glory, like a brash and blatant advertisement, yet it represented a supposedly clandestine group plotting to re-ignite a bloody and tragic war. Its headquarters were by the reeking Thames and its herald was an engraver in Seven Dials whose hand embellished cheap works of bloodthirsty fiction and catchpenny 'fakements' concocted by down and out hacks to be hawked at the foot of the gallows. Suddenly, the Resurgent South enterprise showed itself to be a cheap fraud.

'Mighty stirring stuff, Setty,' commented Dacers with a note of sarcasm. 'All grand and martial.'

Setty Wilkins shrugged. 'Don't mean nothin' to me, Mr. Dacers. It vos just a job, makin' a crust or two. I ain't had no book learnin' — vot does 'resurgent' mean?'

'Don't gammon me, Setty,' said Dacers. 'You have more learning than you let on and you obviously completed a sound apprenticeship to your trade. You write a masterly engravers' copperplate and you never spell a word wrong. As for 'resurgent', in this instance, it means trouble.'

'Trouble don't vorry me,' said Setty. 'In The Dials, ve live in the midst of it all day long and all night. But the coves vot came to see me over the job didn't look much like trouble.'

'How many of them were there?

'Two.'

'Both big men, one with a yellow moustache and a powder burn on his face; the other looking like a prizefighter and both in tall hats and frock coats, all very respectable?' asked Dacers.

'Yes. That's them to a T and it's a great vonder they got in and out of The Dials without having all their valuables lifted as well as their gelt,' replied Setty, using the 'flash' — criminals' slang word for 'money'. He chuckled and added: 'Togged up like they vos, they could easily have been skinned. That means — '

'I know what it means. It's the flash for being robbed of one's clothing and left bare bottom naked. You didn't see anything of a smaller man — a hunch-back?'

'No.'

Fortune might be the brains of the group, thought Dacers, though, it seemed, he contrived to always keep in the background. But there were times when he was decidedly to the fore. He remembered what he saw at the Cardsworth manor house: hump-backed Fortune in the leading role, projecting plans of an improved Southern created submarine boat from a magic lantern and doing all the talking.

The sight of the engraved letterhead caused Dacers' mind to turn to thoughts that first entered it when he crouched in the flower bed under the window of the manor house and heard Fortune's words: *'Whatever you put in will be a sound investment.'* And there was the talk of an eager horde, ready to take up the sword again. Surely, no one could swallow that. One need only read the newspapers to know the South was on its knees.

It was all glib sales talk and, if he ever believed the venture to be a genuine attempt to revive the defeated South into a viable fighting nation by misguided but genuine patriots, he now saw its cheapjack reality.

It was aimed at rooking wealthy British donors, like Sir Oswald Vaillant, who had financed the supply of highly expensive materiel of war to the Southern belligerents. It was an elaborate trick of a kind that might be devised by the intelligent end of the Swell Mob — those of a much brainier order than Dandy Jem and Skinny Eustis.

It was a variation on the mobsmen's confidence dodge known as the 'long firm lurk', whereby money was conjured out of the gullible by setting up a spurious business firm.

Only, in this instance, the gullible were the very rich and Dacers had no idea how many of them had been visited and hooked by their fanciful blather of fortunes to be made.

And, somewhere, Theodore Van Trask fitted into this mosaic of false patriotism, war talk and a hunchback's hump that, according to Miss Van Trask, seemed to come and go.

When he left Setty Wilkins, he was thinking of the Resurgent South or the Dixie Ghosts and the useful knowledge of their address, memorised from the letter-head: *5, Blindman's Yard, Hungerford Bridge*.

So, unless it was merely an address for the reception of mail, it seemed there was a place to which the Dixie Ghosts enterprise could be pinned down.

But he was not the only one concerned with an address.

As Dacers made his way on foot from Seven Dials to Bloomsbury, a solidly built man with a pugnacious face was sitting on a bench in the small park in the centre of the square in which Dacers resided. He ground the butt of a cigar he had just finished under his heel and sighed with boredom.

Sam Meakum had been ordered to keep an eye open for a man who lived at a certain house in the square and, by some means, discover his identity and what his business was.

He had already made the man's acquaintance in a manner of speaking for he was the one he and Cal Tebbutt, who tried to impress the gullible by pretending he was of the aristocratic Virginian

Fairfax clan, had set upon outside the Blue Duck.

He took out his cigar case, selected yet another cigar and lit it with his flint-and-wheel lighter. He made sure he was obscured from view from one side of the square by a tree positioned just behind the bench. Already, the beat policeman had appeared from the edge of the square three times and plodded along that side on his regular, precisely timed patrol.

The peeler had not noticed the solitary man occupying the bench on this cold February day but, sooner or later, he might do so and want to know what Meakum was doing there and why he was lingering so long.

Sam Meakum was considerably disgruntled. He was growing tired of taking orders from the overbearing and fanatically driven Fortune, the deviser of the scheme which, according to Fortune, would net his associates and himself wealth beyond their dreams.

Meakum did not mind pulling his weight in any enterprise. Nor did he mind having to handle the brougham coach the trio had at its disposal because he had a farming background and understood horses. Increasingly, though, he had to take over Cal Tebbutt's duties for the effects of whatever struck Tebbutt over the head in the battle of Shiloh was making him more erratic and unreliable, particularly when he had given in to his passion for hard liquor.

He now considered himself a fool for allowing himself to be pushed by the impetuous Tebbutt into attacking the snooper at the Blue Duck. Moreover, where he normally strove to keep Tebbutt under control, this time, he lost his grip on him and now wondered if he was not being morally contaminated by Tebbutt. Their attack on the snooper yielded nothing. Instead, they should have done their own snooping and followed the man to discover something about him.

More and more, when Fortune was absent from London, supposedly softening up prospective donors to the Resurgent South, Meakum had to handle a dozen jobs and ensure that Cal Tebbutt did not fly off the handle into one of his increasing irrational fits.

The worst so far was the one that caused him to suddenly jump from the carriage in which all three were riding and charge into the home of the U.S. diplomat claiming he had unfinished business there.

At an earlier date, Meakum and Tebbutt had some highly secret business with Theodore Van Trask. That was during the war when Tebbutt and Meakum, as a pair of Southerners stranded in England through the misfortunes of war became associated with Henry Hotze, who was a more or less open Confederate agent. Tebbutt's action the day he barged in on Van Trask stemmed from that business. It was simply crazy and totally fruitless.

Meakum, in the menial role of coach driver, had almost turned the brougham over in making a speedy escape from the scene as Fortune dragged Tebbutt into the coach. It worried Meakum that Tebbutt, whom he had stood by loyally, guarded and helped out through shared vicissitudes, could easily become a liability.

Further concerns worried him He was beginning to doubt the soundness of this Dixie Ghost affair. True, they had visited three or four of the earlier donors of funds to the Confederate cause during the war, but after an initial enthusiasm, they were showing a marked reluctance to make any commitments this time around.

Or was the record of business so meagre because crafty little Fortune was making his own deals during his absences on lone ventures and siphoning off what should be profits for all three? After all, by his own cunning means, Fortune ensured that he always kept on his person the documents and lantern slides used to back up their claims to have the means of creating advanced weapons of war.

Furthermore, he insisted that he and only he should handle all correspondence pertaining to their activities. His two companions were kept in the dark as to how things were progressing and Meakum's feeling they were merely being used as tools was growing.

The more he thought about it the more rickety the Resurgent South or Dixie Ghosts enterprise appeared and his initial enthusiasm for it was being replaced by the feeling that it would not take much to make him up and quit the whole affair. First, though, he must get out of Fortune's clutches. For the hunchback had a tenacious grip and, without his help, Meakum and Tebbutt, as refugees from the broken Confederacy, would be nearly destitute.

Then, suddenly, his gloomy reverie was broken because he saw the very man who was on his mind, crossing the far side of the square. Meakum did not know it but Septimus Dacers was returning from his visit to Setty Wilkins' workshop where he had received his own enlightenment about the Dixie Ghosts affair.

Meakum kept his gaze on the tall figure across the square where he had been joined by the crossing sweeper, one of the ragged legion of London's destitute who earned what they could by sweeping the horse droppings and mud from the cobbles for the well-being of gentlemen's boots and the hems of ladies' gowns as they crossed from kerb to kerb.

He saw the crossing sweeper, a bent old man in an ancient topcoat and a bashed-in old top hat, touch the brim of his headgear then step before the man and begin sweeping with his broom, walking before him and wielding the broom as he crossed. At the further kerb, the man handed the sweeper a tip then walked in the direction of the house whose number Fortune had identified to Meakum. Meakum kept watching until Dacers opened the street door with his key and entered the house. Though he was growing half-hearted about his role in the Dixie Ghost scheme, he set about the task Fortune had set him.

He rose, left the little park and strode across to where the crossing sweeper stood with an idle broom. The old man turned, touched his hat brim and looked hopefully at Meakum but Meakum halted and did not begin to cross the roadway.

Not wanting to leave any evidence of American incursion in the area, Meakum tried to put on a languid English accent.

'Pray, my good fellow, is that gentleman who just crossed the street not Dr. Jones?'

A pair of rheumy eyes, set in an unwashed, grizzled face considered him from under the shattered brim of the stove-in old top hat.

''Im, sir? No, 'e ain't no doctor. That's Mr. Dacers, 'e's a sort of detective like.'

'Oh, a policeman?'

'No, 'e ain't with the reg'lar crushers. 'e's sort of private like. There's bin stories about things wot 'e's done in the noospapers now and then. Not that I could tell you wot they was. Never had no schoolin, d'ye see? Can't read.' He laughed, showing a toothless cavern of a mouth. 'A fair gentleman is Mr. Dacers. I've bin on this crossin' nigh on eight years an' never met a finer gentlemen.' He paused then added meaningfully: ''e allus tips a man 'andsome arter 'e's done a bit of sweepin' for 'im.'

Meakum fished in his pocket, found a sixpence and handed it to the sweeper. 'Thank you,' he said. 'I see I was mistaken. I saw him from a distance and thought he was a Dr. Jones I knew some time ago.' The crossing sweeper touched his hat brim again and Sam Meakum strode off. Now he knew the name of the snooper and what he was — a private detective. Private he might be but that was no guarantee that he was wholly detached from the official police. And he had tailed Meakum and his companions from the Blue Duck to Hertfordshire and back. Who did he represent? Who put him on to their enterprise?

The answers might soon emerge. For Fortune, who had discovered the address of the snooper, had indicated that he had plans for him.

And that thought awakened fears in Sam Meakum. For he knew Fortune to be vicious in ways more sophisticated than the addle-headed Cal Tebbutt. Fortune made sure that almost all his past life was kept a close secret but, from what little he allowed to emerge, Sam Meakum had gleaned that he was a hard case indeed and had indicated that he was not averse to killing. He had the snooping detective, Dacers, on his mind ever since becoming aware of him and had voiced some dark hints as to how he should be dealt with.

But, if Dacers had any connection with the London police and he was disposed of messily, with his killing coming to light, consequences would be dire in the extreme for the Dixie Ghosts.

Meakum was as tough as his pugnacious appearance suggested and not short of courage but he had a healthy attachment to his own skin and had no desire to end his life receiving the fumbling professional services of 'Old Cal' — Mr. William Calcraft, the Crown's frequently drunk-on-duty Public Hangman.

7

At Blindman's Yard

Dacers strode warily among the rubble
and builders' detritus scattered for a good
distance along the river shoreline close to
Hungerford Bridge. It was early evening
and the shades of night were rapidly
descending. The windows, lit by gas and
lantern in the middle distance were
largely those of government offices, by
tradition, established on this northern
side of the river. Not far away was the
headquarters of the Metropolitan Police,
where the back door of the detective
department opened into a small yard
whose name became synonymous with
the department: *Scotland Yard*.

Close to the river's edge, amid the
spreading evidence of Joseph Bazalgette's
huge, ongoing river improvement project,
he was searching for Blindman's Yard. At
first, he blundered among structures

either partially built or partially demolished.

Seemingly, he was quite alone then he was aware that there was someone behind him and a heavy hand dropped on his shoulder causing him to jump. A well known voice boomed: 'Well, Septimus, what're you doing up here in this country?'

Dacers turned and looked into the broad, whisker embellished visage of Detective Inspector Amos Twells, of Scotland Yard. 'Pursuing some complicated riddle, I'll be bound,' declared Twells. 'Is it one you'd care to share with the Yard? After all, we've put a crust or two your way over the years.'

'I'm doing nothing important. Just taking a constitutional.'

'Gammon! The river is no place to take a constitutional. These engineering fellows have done wonderful work but they've yet to properly conquer the great stink,' laughed Twells. 'Care for a pint of ale? There's a quaint little grog shop just a stride away, the Blue Duck, well known to the force. You can enjoy the sight of most of the customers fleeing the moment I show my nose there.'

'No, thank you, I'll continue my walk then think of an early supper.'

'Ah, the excellent Mrs. Slingsby! I'll wager she spoils you with good suppers. Ah, well, enjoy it but I know you're up to something.'

'You're too much the detective, Amos,' said Dacers, trying to sound as light hearted as possible.

Inwardly, he knew he ought to tell Amos Twells what he knew about the Dixie Ghosts although he had only hearsay evidence, gathered by his eavesdropping, and the sight of the engraved letterhead, though he had no knowledge of the literature the group had put out. But his promise to Roberta Van Trask — who thought him such a chivalrous Englishman — had to be honoured. If her father had any role in the affairs of the three Southerners, she wanted to keep Charles Francis Adams and the US Embassy staff in ignorance of it. And that meant saying nothing to the Metropolitan Police.

It was his hope that Theodore Van Trask would ultimately be shown to be clear of any involvement with the Dixie Ghosts, which would leave him free to pass on what he knew to Scotland Yard. For the present, however, he must ensure that he kept his promise to Roberta Van Trask.

Detective Inspector Twells squinted at Dacers' face. Even in the fading light, he could discern the signs of his recent run-in with the two Americans. He nodded and grunted: 'Ah, yes, Septimus, you've been in a mill recently unless you've taken to the bottle and can't keep your legs on course but I know you're not that kind of cove. Well, it's your business, so get on with it.' He moved off in the direction of Scotland Yard where he was due to do a turn of night duty.

Knowing that he could be venturing into certain trouble if any of the three Dixie Ghosts were around, Dacers had taken precautions when his curiosity prompted him to enter their territory. He wore a thick topcoat, a hard, low crowned hat and a muffler to partially hide his face.

142

He walked cautiously through the dark and sinister riverside townscape with its broken buildings, jumble of building materials, idle steam engines of construction and, here and there, attenuated stumps of some of the great, cylindrical pillars which had supported the demolished old Hungerford Bridge created by Isambard Kingdom Brunel. It was haunted by shadows and the eternal stink of the great river.

As he passed the remnants of one of the pillars, a dark clad, black moustached young man, one of two who had been concealed behind it, stepped out and considered his back as he disappeared into the gloom. He quickly returned to the rear of the broken pillar.

'Do you figure he's one of them, Jim?' he asked.

His companion, who had watched the man from his concealment, gave a short laugh.

'No, Irvine. That's an Englishman and I'd stake a fortune on it. You can't live in this country as long as I have and hobnob with Englishmen over all the seven seas without knowing one by the cut of his jib,' said James Bulloch. 'It's a strange thing how you may tell an American, be he Yankee or Southerner, by his style as you may an Englishmen. It's hardly different from telling a ship's nationality by the colours she flies. I don't doubt that man is associated with the building work going on here.'

'Sooner or later, we'll catch sight of them,' said Irvine Bulloch. 'And I hope it's sooner. There's little pleasure in hanging around this locality.'

Septimus Dacers walked over the broken, littered ground with his eyes skinned for Blindman's Yard, blundering into structures partially built or partially demolished. Suddenly, he found it: a cobbled track, slanting upward between the remains of two walls, one of which bore an ancient plaque bearing the words:

'Blindman's Yard.'

In his ample coat pocket he carried what the criminal world called a 'neddy', a short wooden cudgel that could deliver a stunning blow. He had no intention of taking more of the kind of punishment handed out at the Blue Duck by Meakum and Fairfax.

He walked boldly into Blindman's Yard and found it to be a short lane lined with the older type of riverside buildings, which Bazalgette's imaginative project for renewing this portion of London would soon sweep away. In fact, several at the entrance point to the lane had already been reduced to rubble.

Deeper in the deserted lane, eerie and ominous in its quietness, he found a huddle of once black and white timbered buildings, rendered grimy by smoke. Their roofs sagged and slanted crazily and they had probably survived the Great Fire of London of 1666. All were closed up and probably condemned. Faded lettering above the lintels of their doors told of the purposes they once served:

'Ships' *Chandlers,'* *'Pies and Mashed Potatoes', 'Nets and Fishing Tackle,'* 'and *'Barber and Apothecary'.*

He found number five, a building squeezed in among a group of slanting ancient neighbours, its frontage a little cleaner than the rest as if some recent tidying had been done on it to make it look still active.

Like the other premises, it was closed up but a square of paper had been fixed in one of the many paned little windows. Dacers read it:

'RD, Temporary Offices. If closed, kindly leave a message in letter box and a principal will contact you.'

Dacers grinned. So, this was their way of keeping at arm's length from those who might travel to London, seeking their office having seen their letterhead! RD obviously meant 'Resurgent Dixie', but the initials did not convey the full title of the venture to the world at large. Probably, the Dixie Ghosts only visited the place to pick up mail and had established living quarters elsewhere. With the frantic construction work going on all around, they could disarm inquirers with the tale that their permanent offices would be in the new buildings that would rise under Bazalgette's scheme. Their Blindman's Yard premises were indeed temporary and, when all the loot was gathered in, the Dixie Ghosts would decamp from them swiftly and for good.

Night was falling fast, bringing a chill rising from the river. He walked around to the rear of the crouching huddle of buildings and found that their backs faced a narrow, cobbled alley without any form of backyard or enclosure. Small, old-fashioned windows were set in the back walls of the shops.

He was looking at the upper rear windows of number five when he saw the grubby curtain pulled across it suddenly twitch then remain still. So there was somebody in an upper rear room in which there was no light! And he was pretty sure that there was enough natural illumination in the alley for him to be visible to the watcher. He slipped his hand into his pocket and took a tight grip on the neddy.

Just as he began to make a discreet exit

from the alley, Dacers heard the scrape of boots at one end of it. He turned and saw two dark and bulky figures bearing down on him — Meakum and the man who called himself Fairfax were coming at him with determined strides.

Another footfall from the opposite end of the alley caused him to turn his head and he saw the small shape of a humped man — Fortune — coming just as determinedly. Having seen him from the rear window, they must have left the shop by its front door then walked around the opposite ends of the tumbledown block to enter either end of the alley. Dacers took the neddy from his pocket and prepared to use it. The three had him cornered in the confined space of the narrow alleyway and they were clearly out for trouble. He was up against bigger odds than at the Blue Duck but he was determined he would not take the pounding he took on that painful occasion.

For the first time, he had a good look at Fortune who was now very close to him. Even in the poor light, the hunchback had a memorable face: lantern jawed with high cheekbones and remarkable glittering eyes beneath thickly grown brows. He could quite see why Roberta Van Trask could not believe there were two men with the same face and the hunchback she glimpsed in London was the man without a hump, seen in Washington.

Fortune sprang at him with an agility astonishing in one with a spinal infirmity.

'Damn, you!' he snarled. 'You're going to get your hash settled for good and all.'

He clawed for Dacers' throat just as Dacers swung the neddy. He contacted with the side of Fortune's head, knocking him to one side and, within the same split second, Fortune's two henchmen grabbed him from behind.

They hauled him backwards on his heels but he twisted out of their grip, lashed out blindly with the neddy and smote Meakum across the nose, bringing a gurgle of pain from him. Then grasping hands seemed to come out of the gloom as the trio clutched at him at the same time, barging into him with their combined weight. Again, as in the assault at the Blue Duck, he noticed the strong aroma of whisky from one of the attackers.

His knees buckled and he went down to the cobbles. All three men piled on top of him and, gasping for breath, he was almost crushed by their bodies. He wriggled and squirmed against the combined pressure and, still with the neddy in his grasp, he tried to free his arm to use the weapon but he was pinned down too tightly. He somehow managed to work his left arm free of the pressure and launched his bunched fist into the thick of the melee, making satisfying contact with someone's mouth.

His assailants piled more pressure on him and one hit him a dizzying blow across the head. Suddenly, he was being hauled up to his feet. He tried to swing the neddy into action but a fist hit his upper arm and seized the short cudgel, snatching it out of his grasp. Now he was standing, held up by the three.

His hat was gone, and he was almost totally winded but he still tried to find the energy to kick at the legs of the trio as they began to manhandle him, forcing him against the back wall of the row of shops.

Then, a speedily delivered rabbit punch to the back of the neck momentarily stunned him. It was swiftly followed by a fist crashing against the side of his head and the whole murky world of Blindman's Yard closed in on him as he lost consciousness.

His senses came swimming up out of darkness he knew not how long after the attack. He was aware that he was lying on rough boards and that he was indoors in a dimly lit room. The air was musty and, as his head cleared, Dacers focussed his eyes on a point of light some distance off. It resolved itself into a window, covered with a curtain through which an uncertain illumination, possibly the early dawn, filtered.

Slowly, it came to him that this was the window he saw from the alleyway from which someone watched him. He was therefore in the upper back room of the old shop in which the Dixie Ghosts had set up their headquarters.

A grating voice, which he recognised as

that of Fortune said: 'He's conscious. Throw some water over him!'

Somebody moved and clumped off over creaking floorboards. A couple of minutes later, he returned and a spout of icy water was dashed in his face. He spluttered, shook his head and realised that three partially perceived figures were squatting beside him.

'Mr. Dacers, the detective,' it was Fortune's Southern drawl again. 'We're haunted by you, my friend, but not for much longer. You've followed us for the last time and we're going to be good and rid of you. First, who's behind you? Who put you on to us? Are you tied up with anybody from the U.S. Embassy?'

Dacers struggled to find his voice. When it came it was a dry croak but he managed to make it defiant: 'Nothing to say.'

Fortune snorted. 'Really? I guess we'll see about that in due course. Meantime, thanks for walking into our hands the way you did, saving us a deal of trouble. We know a lot about you, Dacers. We know where you live, for instance, and would you believe that my colleagues and I spent a deal of time figuring out means of grabbing you as you left your house but there are several snags in your square during the daylight hours. There are too many potential witnesses: the policeman on the beat; the old crossing sweeper and the cabmen who hang around the cab stand at the further end of the square. Not much chance of grabbing you at night, either, short of breaking in and snatching you from your bed but that would be too hazardous. Then you came to us right off your own bat — so very obliging.'

Dacers was wondering how Fortune knew his name and, at the same time was trying to think up an answer to his gloating monologue. His thoughts became dominated by Roberta Van Trask and the need to save her father from whatever it was that he feared and was certainly connected with these men in some way. He made a steely resolution that he would not reveal to them anything he knew about their scheming or anything about himself.

Fortune had only paused for breath and he began to speak again in his languid Southern drawl: 'We have plans for you, Mr. Dacers, real plans, not the half-baked efforts of our Mr. Tebbutt, here, who would have you believe he's a blue blooded Fairfax. He figured the tide would carry you away when it rose after he almost tipped you into the river but had it all wrong. Mr. Tebbutt, I fear, is too fond of hard liquor and, because it impairs his thinking, he frequently goes wrong.' Fortune, it seemed was very much out of sorts with Tebbutt who claimed to be a Virginian aristocrat.

'Hell, I only had a couple of drinks,' complained one of the shadowy figures squatting alongside Fortune.

'Two too many,' rejoined Fortune sharply. 'That's the trouble with putting up at Josh Tooley's saloon. The liquor's too close at hand. Well, there'll be no fumbling this time. It's the river for you, Mr. Dacers.'

'Have a care,' interjected Meakum with a nervous quiver in his voice. 'We know he's a detective. He's sure to be friendly with the London coppers. If he's found in the river right here in the heart of the city, there'll be an all-fired hue and cry. The Limey authorities will make gallows meat of us in no time.'

'Stop bellyaching,' growled Tebbutt. 'You were just the blamed same at the Blue Duck, squawkin' with the jitters when I suggested putting him in the river.'

'Only you were too damned stupid to drop him into the river. You merely dumped him on a mudbank,' growled Fortune disdainfully. 'Well it won't be like that this time. We won't put him in here. He'll go in further upstream, in the country and very well weighted. He'll never be found among all the reeds and weeds out that way.'

He leaned forward, bringing his face closer to Dacers' and the improving morning light creeping through the grubby window showed his fanatically glittering eyes. 'You can be assured it'll be a boss job, with no half measures. If I put him in the river, he'll stay with the fishes for good and all.'

Dacers was trying to put his thoughts into order. He had just learned that the Dixie Ghosts were staying at the Blue Duck so, probably, they had simply commandeered this empty old shop to use as a front for their operation. A cynical part of his brain told him it was all very well to collect information on his opponents but it would be of no use if he was at the bottom of the Thames.

The light from the window strengthened and Dacers saw the faces of the three, squatting beside him: Tebbutt, looking surly; pugnacious faced Meakum, a picture of discontent and plainly troubled and Fortune, with stark malevolence in his glittering eyes and murder in his heart.

Dacers felt an aching stiffness creeping into his body and, for the first time, he discovered that his hands were tied behind his back and he was lying on them. He wondered if his captors were going to kill him there and then either by shooting or bludgeoning him and then disposing of his corpse. Or would they gag him, attach weights and throw him into the river while alive?

Neither prospect appealed to him and caused him to wriggle and attempt to loosen the bonds tightened around his wrists. Fortune noticed his struggles and, with a frosty grin, he snarled: There's no point in struggling, Mr. Dacers, you're tied up pretty firmly and that's the way you'll stay until what's left of you is found on the riverbed some distant day from now.'

He rose to his feet and his two henchmen followed suit. Fortune nodded curtly to Tebbutt.

'C'mon, you,' he ordered. 'We're going to the Blue Duck to get Josh Tooley's brougham ready to take Mr. Dacers out to the country where the lovely Thames flows so sweetly. I need you to help with the rig and you will not touch a bubble of liquor while you're at the saloon. We have serious business on hand.'

Dacers made another mental note — not only did the Dixie Ghosts lodge under the roof of the Blue Duck but the hostelry's landlord was the owner of the carriage they used. Josiah Tooley was evidently very much tied up with the Dixie Ghosts. Then, the chilling thought returned: what was the earthly use of collecting evidence and holding it in his head when he was about to be killed without a chance of using it?

Fortune addressed Meakum: 'You stay here, since you're so stricken by conscience and seem to have no belly for what we're about to do. You can guard Mr. Dacers. He's been struggling pretty damned hard to get free of those ropes. Make sure he doesn't manage it. And be just as sure that Mr. Dacers is going to be disposed of my way no matter how many high principled objections you make.'

Dacers, lying on the coarse, dusty boards of the floor, had a chance to take in his surroundings now that the light of day, struggling through the grubby curtain, was stronger. It was sparsely fitted out with some oddments of decrepit furniture, which must have been there for decades. There were a few plates, cups and eating utensils and items of clothing scattered about, suggesting that the trio used this place as a bolthole, situated as it was in a deserted and abandoned region in the midst of the extensive improvement workings. The Dixie Ghosts were lodging at the Blue Duck but that was probably too public a place for them to spend too much time there in the ordinary course of the day so this closed-up old shop was an obscure place in which they could hatch their plots.

He kept his eyes half closed, as if still partially stunned but, watching through slitted lids, he saw Fortune and Tebbutt, putting on their tall hats, preparing to go out. Fortune issued orders to his companion: 'We'll go out by the back way and keep to the alleys. Some of these building people might be hanging around and we don't want them to get too nosey,' he stipulated. He turned to Meakum, saying curtly: 'Keep a tight watch on this fellow until we get the brougham here to drive him out to the country.'

Meakum merely looked at him and glowered darkly while Dacers' thoughts raced. From what he had just heard, it seemed it was Fortune's intention to kill him where they were at that moment, then drive his corpse out to the country to dispose of it in the upper waters of the Thames. That way lessened the chances of his bloated remains floating up to the surface of the river in the thickly populated surroundings of the city, as frequently happened, so setting off an inquiry.

Fortune opened the warped old door of the room, which gave a harsh protesting creak and he and Tebbutt left.

Sam Meakum sat on an unsafe looking old chair and waited until he heard the slam of the shop's rear door sounding from below. Then, deliberately, he stood up, slipped a hand inside his waistcoat and produced a long, broad bladed Bowie knife. The sight of it brought an icy whirligig swirling in Dacers' innards as he remembered the ugly knife used by the swell mobsman, Dandy Jem, and the injury he suffered when he assisted Twells in arresting Jem.

Frowning, with his mouth tightened into a grim line of determination and gripping the knife purposefully, Meakum advanced on the helplessly bound Dacers.

8

Pursuit

Sam Meakum crouched over Dacers with the knife in his hand. Dacers, lying on his back with his hands tightly bound under him held his breath as he saw the uncertain light put a sheen on the broad blade which, in its design, seemed to reflect the crudity and savagery of the American frontier where it was devised. He saw beads of perspiration on Meakum's fleshy face and heard his gasping, anxious breathing. He showed all the signs of a man in a hurry.

'Turn over!' barked Meakum. 'C'mon, quick turn over!'

Dacers, stiff through lying in such an unnatural position for so long, wriggled and made slow work of turning his body over and Meakum urged again in a voice edged with desperate urgency: 'C'mon, turn over, damn you. I want to cut those ropes!'

Bewildered, Dacers tried to find an answer but, with his face against the filthy boards of the floor, he could only manage an incoherent gurgle.

He felt Meakum grab his hands in his own big hands, then the knife began to slice into the ropes and he felt them slackening. Blood began to circulate in his aching hands and wrists again.

'I'm getting the hell out,' said Meakum with the same breathless suggestion of panic in his voice. 'I ain't going to be a party to killing you. I'm running for it before those two get back here — and you do the same, damn quick. Don't underestimate Fortune.'

'What the — '

'No questions. I haven't time. Nor have you. I'm skeedadling, getting away from Fortune and that half crazy drunk, Cal Tebbutt who thinks he can fool the Limey quality by borrowing the name of Virginia quality and can't see that Fortune's just using him. I'm sick of the whole blamed fool game and I'm damned if I'll stoop to murder and finish at the end of a rope.

C'mon, quick. On your feet!'

Dacers, with his hands free, was hauled up to a standing position by Meakum.

And he realised that the pugnacious, solidly built man was quivering like a jelly obviously consumed by fear and in a desperate hurry to get away.

Questions crowded into Dacer's mind. He wanted to ask about the scheme the three were operating and about the attack on Theodore Van Trask and much more but Meakum gave him no opportunity. He shoved Dacers to one side forcefully, grabbed his hat from where he had left it beside the chair he sat in and crammed it on his head with one hand while stowing the knife under his coat with the other.

He made for the door at speed. He was in a near blind panic at the prospect of the imminent return of his erstwhile partners in the Dixie Ghosts scheme. He turned and said hoarsely: 'Get out, quick. Back way's the quickest, the door's already open. They'll bring the coach into the alley, so get out before they show up!'

He pulled the door open with a groan of hinges and fled from the room. Then there came the echoing sound of his feet clattering down the bare boards of a stairway.

Dacers was utterly stunned by this turn of events. He was not to know that Meakum had long been uneasy about the Resurgent South project and his part in it. While numerous former contributors to the Confederate States' coffers during the war showed an initial interest in the proposal the Dixie Ghosts were hawking, second thoughts seemed to have won out. Few followed up with a definite decision to risk more funds on the dream of a reborn Confederacy.

That, at least, was the state of affairs as reported to his two colleagues by Fortune. His insistence that he alone had the right to deal with all paperwork, including such little mail as arrived at the closed-up old shop premises in Blindman's Yard which served as their front plus his caginess in giving any detailed account of the progress of the enterprise forced Meakum to the conviction that Fortune was cheating. He suspected he was diverting whatever money materialised into his personal channels. When pressed for an evaluation of progress, Fortune always took the disarming line that things were bound to be slow at first but the assured fortune would eventually arrive.

Meakum's sudden flight left Dacers standing blank-minded for a couple of minutes, rubbing his rope-chafed wrists. Then the chilling import of Meakum's warning hit him — Fortune and Tebbutt were about to show up with the coach. Their intention was murder; Dacers was to be the victim and the coach would carry him to the place where his corpse would be disposed of.

The thought of it jarred him into action and he charged through the door, found himself on a decrepit landing from which a flight of unsafe looking warped wooden stairs descended. A musty smell of rot and decay permeated the innards of the building. Dacers clattered down the stairs, moving as fast as he could and fearing that the whole structure might collapse under his weight. He reached the bottom and was in a narrow hallway. An open door revealed what had obviously once been a kitchen and a splash of daylight within it indicated the open back door through which, doubtless, Meakum had fled into the rear alley.

Dacers ran for the light and came out of the gloom and the reek of decay into the alley and the light of full day, bright but edged by the icy nip of winter.

He looked around, seeing no sign of Meakum. The mean alley was totally deserted as was so much of this region where the Bazalgette reconstruction project was in progress. A row of the rear of closed up shops similar to that from which Dacers had just emerged made up the opposite side of the alley; floored with broken cobbles

Still half bewildered and feeling one of the twinges in his wound which Dr McLeish warned him about, Dacers looked about him, wondering which way to run and decided to go to his left. To go right would be to travel towards the Blue Duck and it was from that direction that the coach would be coming.

With his heart thumping, Dacers raced for the further end of the alley. He was intent on getting clear of this place but a portion of his mind was trying to think ahead. Should he now go to Scotland Yard? It was difficult to be sure of what hard evidence there was against the Dixie Ghosts to present to the police. Possibly attempting to obtain money by deception; attempted fraud and conspiracy to murder could be levelled against them, but what was the weight of proof?

Pounding the cobbles of the alley with his legs moving like pistons, his thoughts whirled around another issue. He had to escape the murderous pair. At the same time, he needed to confront Fortune physically. For he now had vital knowledge about the man that should go a long way to exposing the Dixie Ghosts. Implementing it required physical action. He had to physically get his hands on the hunchback.

Abruptly, his striving to sift out his difficulties while running was halted. Turning into the alley directly ahead of him and fully in his path was the brougham carriage with Tebbutt at the reins and, probably, Fortune inside. There was only just room in the narrow alley for the vehicle. Dacers had fully expected it to return by way of the other end of the alley since that was the direction in which the Blue Duck lay. Into his alarmed thoughts came the notion that, outside the approaches to Blindman's Yard, there must be many obstacles such as partially demolished buildings and stacks of materials because of the improvement works, that Fortune and Tebbutt were forced to make a detour which meant they had to enter the alley at its other end.

Septimus Dacers, with his heart in his mouth, saw the brougham looming in front of him and he felt bottled up in the narrow ribbon of the alley. Tebbutt only had to urge speed out of the horse to send the animal and carriage hurtling forward to knock him over, trample him and run the wheels over him.

Tebbutt half stood behind the reins and Dacers was now close enough to him to see distinctly his mouth dropping open and his eyes widening with surprise. He yelled in alarm: 'Dacers is free!' His voice had the near hysterical quiver Dacers had noted before.

Almost in mid-stride, when he seemed to be near enough to touch the horse's nose, Dacers whirled around and began to run back the other way. When in the very act of turning, he saw Fortune's head protrude out of the carriage window while, over the clop of hoofs and the rumble of iron-rimmed wheels on uneven cobbles, Tebbutt was bawling again: 'Dacer's is free! He's out!'

Dacers turned his head briefly while he tried to put on a spurt of speed. He seemed to be barely a yard ahead of the pursuing coach and Fortune's head was out of the window. It looked hardly inches away from the backs of the buildings hemming in his side of the alley. His hand appeared and the wintery morning sunshine touched a gleam to it. A revolver!

Trying to run at a crouch and feeling a jab of pain in his recently healed side, Dacers gritted his teeth, expecting at any second to feel either a bullet slamming into his back or to be flattened and pulped by a surging weight of horseflesh and carriage.

The revolver barked, sounding like a cannon in the restricted space of the alley. A bullet screamed somewhere near the back of Dacer's head and ricocheted off one of the walls. Obviously, there was so little space between the window of the coach and the side of the alley racing past Fortune that he could could hardly aim straight but Dacers might not be so lucky if Fortune fired again.

Suddenly, Dacers was at the end of the alley and was aware of a confusion of urgent sounds at his back: the hoarse voice of Tebbutt crying for the horse to stop; the animal's protests and the grinding of iron on the cobbles and an incoherent gurgle from Fortune.

He realised that the carriage was being forced to halt and when he burst out of the alley, he saw why. The immediate outside area was littered with the debris of shattered buildings, piles of materials, temporary wooden structures and idle steam diggers and cranes associated with Joseph Bazalgette's ambitious Thames improvement work. A coach could not progress through it, which was why it was forced to detour and enter the alley by its further end.

Dacers, panting heavily, with leaden legs and a niggling throb in his wounded side, conjectured that, in carrying out their intended murderous plan, the Dixie Ghosts, after putting him, dead or alive, into the coach, would be forced to the tricky expedient of backing the brougham and horse out of the alley because there was no room to turn and no other way out.

Abruptly, there came a screeching of wheels on cobblestones, a grinding of metal and the sound of shattering wood, the frightened neighing of a horse and the mingled curses of two men. He threw a quick backward glance at his pursuers and saw that the brougham had swerved and hit one wall of the narrow passage-way and was now slanted across the alley, one wheel having broken. An agitated Tebbutt was helping Fortune out of the tilted body of the coach.

Dacers, ebbing strength, burst out of the mouth of the alley, Tebbutt and Fortune, he thought, would be occupied with their difficulties with the horse and coach for some time. They might, however, show themselves at any moment and he was fearful of Fortune's revolver and Tebbutt's Derringer. He plunged, half staggering into the maze of material scattered over a wide area between Blindman's Yard and the river.

Physically weary through his recent exertions on top of the night's loss of sleep, he blundered around among piles of stone in the middle of which stood a temporary wooden shed, seemingly locked up. There was no evidence of any of Bazalgette's workmen in this location. He lurched into the lee of the shed and sank down to sit on the ground and recover his breath. Sheltered there, he could see nothing of the alleyway behind the old shops of Blindman's Yard.

He had lost his low crowned hat and his neddy, though it would hardly be any defence against the firearms carried by

Fortune and Cal Tebbutt.

Although he was only a few yards from the opening of the alley from which those two might appear at any moment, tiredness caused him to drop his guard. His eyes closed and he fell into a half doze. He was jarred back to startled consciousness by the scrape of boots and the sound of voices, which, ominously, had the slow, drawling quality of the Southern American states.

'This fellow could be one of them,' stated one voice.

'No, he's the Englishman we saw last night,' said a deeper and older voice. 'I told you, Irvine, I can spot an Englishman anywhere.'

Dacers became fully awake and found two figures wearing heavy topcoats against the February cold and tall hats were standing over him. One was youngish with a bar of dark moustache and the other was older with a rich crop of facial whiskers.

'He might be English, Jim, but he could still be one of them,' said the younger man. 'We don't know how many of them there are or what nationalities are involved.'

As Dacers began to rise, the younger man grabbed him and hauled him up, bringing him out from behind the shed. Now, all three were standing within full view of the alley from which Fortune and Tebbutt had not emerged to pursue Dacers.

Holding Dacers by the coat collar, the younger man demanded roughly: 'Are you involved with the Resurgent South outfit?'

Dacers mouth dropped open at the sound of the name of the confidence trick and a question whirled through his mind: who were this pair from America and what was their involvement with the Dixie Ghosts?

He tried to form a reply but before he could do so, Tebbutt and Fortune emerged from the opening of the alley and Fortune had his revolver in his hand. He stopped dead in his tracks when he saw Dacers standing with the two intruders a few yards away in the midst of the building materials. His eyes became as wide as dollar pieces and took on a more intense glitter than usual. They were focussed on the younger of the two men who was gripping Dacers' collar: 'Lieutenant Bulloch!' he almost gasped the name as if winded by surprise.

Dacers felt the man's grip on his collar loosen and experienced his own jolt of surprise at hearing the man named. Bulloch was the name of the very active and elusive Southern agent in Liverpool in connection with whom he had visited the city as bodyguard to Theodore Van Trask during the American war.

The man with the black moustache stared at Fortune as if in total disbelief then found his voice: 'Mr. Fortune, of all people!' he exclaimed. 'Mr. Fortune!' Then he seemed to be enlightened and make a connection between Fortune and the Resurgent South about which he had asked Dacers shortly before. He framed the question again: 'Fortune, are you — ?'

Fortune appeared to be rooted to the spot for a brief spell, but clearly anticipated how the question would finish. His squat frame quivered and he brought up the revolver as if to shoot Lieutenant Bulloch.

Bulloch, seeming to be mesmerised by the discovery of Fortune, paid no attention to the levelled weapon. A year and a half before, he had faced the United States' warship *Kearsarge*, bearing down on the raider *Alabama* with all guns blazing to send her to the bottom of the English Channel. Compared with that experience, facing one man with a mere pistol seemed as nothing. He continued walking towards Fortune with the older Bulloch following him and the weary Dacers bringing up the rear.

Lieutenant Irvine Bulloch was bewildered and surprised at meeting Fortune, whom he knew as a guest in the officers' mess aboard the *Shenandoah*. Equally surprised at finding him with a levelled gun in his hand, he was surprised most of all by the discovery that this supposed loyal Dixie patriot was somehow a party to a fraudulent criminal venture that cynically misused the defeated South and its stricken people in its web of lies.

Aboard the *Shenandoah*, Fortune told

the officers little about himself except that he was an official of the Confederate government with a role that had to be kept highly secret. He had escaped from Richmond when the rebel capital fell, he was charged by President Jefferson Davis himself to go to England, carrying vital documents and connect with friends of the South there who could help in alleviating the sufferings of the defeated people.

Fleeing from the crushed South by devious ways, he had become stranded in the Azores.

The Bullochs had broken their Liverpool cover and travelled to London as a matter of honour to get to the bottom of the obvious fraud that lay behind the letter they saw. They found the closed up shop premises in its derelict setting the very appearance of which confirmed the bogus status of the self-styled Dixie Ghosts. Now, within reach of two of the scheme's perpetrators, they seemed not to be intimidated by Fortune's revolver just as they had never been intimidated by powerful enemy naval guns on the high seas.

'Get back!' snarled Fortune. 'Get back, damn you, or I'll shoot!'

He continued backing away with Cal Tebbutt beside him doing the same. Fear was beginning to take hold of Tebbutt. His mental balance was precarious at the best of times and it was slipping in the face of the three determined men advancing on Fortune and himself. They seemed to embody retribution, revenge and a settling of accounts. His instinct was to go for his Derringer but it was concealed within his heavy winter clothing and a form of paralysis was preventing him from fumbling for it.

Fortune's courage was holding up no better. The gun was beginning to shake in his hand as the trio came closer to his companion and himself. He did not know who or what they represented. He knew who Irvine Bulloch was and he knew that Dacers, whom he had plotted to kill, was a private detective but who was the older, bulkier man with them? Was he one of the dogged policemen from Scotland Yard?

A worm of logic wriggled its way

through the panicky confusion in Fortune's mind, telling him that he dare not shoot. He had already fired one shot after Dacers in the alley and it seemed not to have alarmed this derelict region, which was being used as a storage area for the river improvement works. However, with the working day now starting, gangs of men would be working not far away. To open fire on the three men would be to attract immediate attention and bring a crowd of the curious and, quite probably, the police.

The indecision and fear of Tebbutt and himself was obvious to the menacing trio and served to embolden them. They continued to advance with firmer steps. Fortune's gun hand began to shake more noticeably and he voiced a jittery and feeble warning: 'Get back! Get back, damn you or I'll shoot!'

He and Tebbutt continued to back away and the two Bullochs and Dacers followed them, step by step. Then, with lightning speed remarkable in one with a physical impairment, Fortune suddenly turned and ran off into the midst of the building materials, engines and huts arrayed along the margin of the Thames. This caused Cal Tebbutt, alongside him, to shake off the grip of fear and he whirled around and joined Fortune in flight.

The fleeing pair began to thread their way through the scattered confusion of the expansive storage site and the Bullochs charged after them. Septimus Dacers, wearied to the bone as he was, managed to find the energy and wakefulness to run after them. He desperately wanted to get his hands on Fortune and was willing to risk a bullet if Fortune should turn and fire on his pursuers.

Almost miraculously, the chase and the sheer desire to catch Fortune caused Dacers to find new energy and he overtook the Bullochs, putting on a spurt of speed as Fortune and Tebbutt somehow keeping together, swerved around a pile of timber. Ahead of them was a cleared space and the curtailed remains of one of the huge classical pillars of the old Hungerford Bridge designed by Brunel.

Fortune and Tebbutt were level with

the pillar when Tebbutt stumbled and fell but Dacers continued running, gaining on Fortune who was showing signs of wearying. Just as he reached the pillar, Dacers caught up with him, lunged forward in a dive and gripped him about the waist. They both smote the earth at the foot of the pillar. Fortune's revolver flew out of his hand and skittered across the ground.

Somewhere in the background, sounds of scuffling, grunts and occasional yelps indicated that Tebbutt was being roughly handled by the Bullochs.

Dacers and Fortune sprawled in the dirt with Dacers clutching the hunch-back's legs and Fortune trying to fight him off. They rolled around at the base of the remnant of the huge pillar, panting and snarling. Dacers found he was close to the fallen revolver. He flung out his arm and grabbed the weapon by its barrel then waved it, clublike, over Fortune's head.

'Keep still or I'll knock you cold!' he spluttered through a mouthful of dirt.

Fortune, panting and growling, continued to struggle and Dacers managed to shove him against the remains of the pillar where his energy gave out. He heaved a gusting sigh and lay still, fighting for breath.

Dacers rose from sprawling to his knees and held the pistol threateningly over Fortune's head. He now had the man totally at his mercy. 'You're keeping a big secret, Mr. Fortune, but not for much longer,' he stated triumphantly.

The younger Bulloch left his brother sitting on the sprawling and defeated Tebbutt and joined Dacers to be greeted with a strange request. 'Help me get his clothes off,' said Dacers, struggling with the buttons of Fortune's heavy top coat.

'What?'

'Help me get his coat off — and his waistcoat and shirt,' repeated Dacers. Fortune was lying on his back and struggling feebly but seeming almost exhausted while Dacers opened his coat buttons.

'Go easy on him,' cautioned the naval man, 'remember he has a disability.'

'Disability be damned. Help me with this waistcoat,' rejoined Dacers. They removed the waistcoat then set about

Fortune's shirt, which Dacers fairly tore off.

Then Irvine Bulloch stared and gasped. For the true nature of Fortune's 'disability' was revealed.

Secured by an arrangement of straps going over his shoulders and under his arms, the hump on his back was shown to be a cleverly shaped rigid mound made of leather which, under clothing, gave the exact impression of being a malformation of the spine.

Fortune's hump was as fraudulent as the get-rich-quick venture he promoted.

9

Debacle

'By thunder!' exclaimed Irvine Bulloch.
'He's not a hunchback at all!'

'I guessed he wasn't some time ago,'
said Dacers, trying to supress a grin of
satisfaction. 'I heard a suggestion that the
hump seemed to appear and disappear
now and again. These two and their
henchman jumped on me in the alley at
Blindman's Yard last night and caught me
after a tussle. During the fight, I
happened to grab Fortune's hump and
felt the whole thing shift under my hands
and I knew it was not a natural part of his
body.'

Fortune, whose face was being held
down on the ground, wriggled and
grumbled and snarled as the pair
examined the leather hump.

It had an opening, a kind of door,
securely fastened with a clasp, and the

device was clearly a form of case or satchel.

'Forget the shop at Blindman's Yard. That's only a place for mail delivery. This is the real office of the Dixie Ghosts,' declared Dacers. He opened the aperture, put his hand inside and produced several papers and some square, flat packages.

'What are those?' asked Irvine Bulloch.

'Correspondence which Fortune guarded jealously. These letters should reveal if these rascals made any money from their confidence trick. I suppose others are lists of the British donors to the war funds of the Confederacy, to be approached for more money.'

'Yes,' said Irvine Bulloch as if suddenly enlightened, 'Fortune came into this country with us aboard the *Shenandoah*. He claimed to be a government official given a last secret mission by Jefferson Davis and was carrying special papers.'

He pushed Fortune's head, squeezing his face against the ground.

'I suppose you did have some kind of government post in Richmond, Mr.

Fortune,' he said 'and you managed to make away with useful papers when the Confederacy collapsed.'

'Go to hell!' croaked Fortune with difficulty. 'I'm telling you nothing!

Dacers opened one of the square packages and examined the contents.

'As I thought, these packages contain the slides for the wonderful magic lantern contraption which they showed to their dupes. They'll show the plans of what are supposed to be spectacular new weapons of war which need financing — and all are bogus. I suppose Fortune managed to have them made after leaving Richmond.'

Irvine Bulloch blew out his cheeks. 'I thought he was a genuine hunchback but he carried this thing on his back day in and day out!'

'Can you think of a better way of safeguarding your papers and other things, including items you need to perpetrate fraud, especially when you're on the move most of the time, visiting the prospects you hope to dupe?' Dacers said.

'Who are you, by the way? Police?' asked Irvine Bulloch

'Dacers, a private inquiry agent, not official police. And I know you're Bulloch. I have reason to remember a Bulloch who was doing a particular service for the Confederate States in Liverpool during the American war.'

'That was my brother who is keeping the other gentleman company just behind us,' said the younger Bulloch. 'And if you ever have any dealings with the United States' Embassy, we'd take it as a great favour if you never mention knowing us or seeing us in London.'

Dacers nodded. 'Of course. A matter hanging over from your big war, I take it.'

'Yes,' said Irvine Bulloch with a wry grin. 'Hanging is exactly the word. Charges of piracy, but that's as much as I'm saying.'

'My lips are sealed,' Dacers assured him. 'Speaking of the United States' Embassy, I must have a word or two with Mr. Tebbutt, over there, whom your brother is using as a seat.' Fortune, whom the pair were holding down, began to make the most coherent remarks he could, considering his face was pressed hard against the earth. Mostly, they were lurid curses.

'I suspect,' said Dacers 'back in America, this hump came and went depending on which side of the Potomac River you happened to be, Mr. Fortune, the side held by the Union or the one held by the Confederacy.'

'Who told you that?' spluttered Fortune with poison in his voice.

'Oh, a most reliable party recalled that you were friendly with a certain Union officer when you were on the Washington side of the river — a Colonel Baker, I understand, and you were without a hump when with him. I'm willing to bet that when you crossed the river to the rebel side, you changed character and became a hunchback. I suppose some clever disguise, a crop of false whiskers perhaps, made you a different man from the one known across the river. Is it possible that what you learned on the Southern side went into your hump to be passed on to Colonel Baker and what you learned on the Northern side went to the Southern intelligence men — for money in both cases, of course. Were you a double agent, Mr. Fortune?'

'Damn you!' growled Fortune and, in spite of being held down by the two men, he suddenly became voluble. 'And why not? I'm a Southerner but with no allegiance to either side. I didn't care who was right or wrong in the war. I cared about me and what I could make out of it. I did work for the Confederate government for a short time and I knew where records of the dealings with the British individuals and firms were kept. I made sure I got hold of them when the government fell and some offices were abandoned as the Yankee army took Richmond.'

Dacers left the sinewy Irvine Bulloch firmly pressing the defeated Fortune to the ground and approached James Bulloch, a man of weight and some girth, who was sitting on the subdued Cal Tebbutt.

'Commander Bulloch, it's an honour to meet you, sir.' he greeted. 'I know something of your record in Liverpool and, as a neutral, I think I'm permitted to say your enterprise and skill in obtaining vessels for your country were admirable,' Dacers said.

James Bulloch looked up from his unusual seat, gave Dacers a genial nod and said in a rich Georgia accent: 'Thank you, sir, but it was all in the line of duty for a simple sailor. What are we to do with this fellow, another renegade Southerner who would use the plight of his stricken people to fill his pockets?'

'There are some things he and his companions, one of whom is missing, are answerable to British law for: attempting to obtain money by false pretences or perhaps outright fraud if they've obtained any money,' Dacers said. 'And there's conspiracy to commit murder. A charge in which I'm personally interested. I also have a most particular interest in knowing what went on between him and a certain gentleman attached to the United States' Embassy.'

Cal Tebbutt looked up from under James Bulloch's bulk. The blue powder burn on his face was vivid blue against skin white from fear. 'You mean old Van

Trask!' he spat. 'Well, I can tell you he's a traitor to his country! He gave money to the Confederate States — and I'm saying no more — except that he owes me money!'

Dacers had not realised it but other people were coming on to the scene. Half a dozen roughly clad working men from the renovation project had drifted into this location where the materials of their occupation were stored. They were led by a large, full bearded man with clenched fists as big as hams. He had a firm step and an angry scowl.

''ere, what're you blokes doin' 'ere?' He demanded loudly. 'I'm foreman on this section an' you've no right to be 'ere. What's the game? Been some sort of a mill, 'as there? Two coves lyin' on the ground and the rest of you lookin' like you're up to no good!' He looked at the brothers Bulloch who had now left Fortune and Tebbutt sprawled on the ground. Throughout all the action, the Bullochs had managed to retain their tall hats, which, with their dark topcoats, still gave them an appearance of dignity. ''an a couple of toffs among you!' shouted the foreman. 'If you don't 'ook it quick, I'll get my blokes to set about you!'

More workmen were drifting in and joining the initial group and a small crowd was gathering. The woebegone Tebbutt was now standing groggily and Dacers dragged the half-clad Fortune to his feet and took a firm grip on the false hump with its contents of evidence.

He turned to the scowling foreman to attempt to give some sort of explanation when he noticed that the Bullochs had slipped away from the scene, using the crowd as cover.

He knew the reason why. James Bulloch, because of his commissioning of commerce raiders in Liverpool during the Civil War and Irvine Bulloch, because he was an officer aboard the raider *Alabama*, were designated pirates by the United States' government. They had a safe hiding place in Liverpool but, here in London, if they were to be captured and taken to the United States' Embassy, they would be on American soil where warrants could be served. They would be deported for trial in America. This was a matter in which Dacers must keep his promise to Irvine Bulloch. From now on, he had not seen the Bulloch brothers.

Just as he faced the angry bearded face of the foreman, Dacers was startled by a well-known voice bellowing behind him: 'Dacers! What's the row here?'

He jerked his head round to see Detective Inspector Amos Twells, accompanied by two large men in civilian clothes, very obviously detectives, bearing down on him.

Amos Twells stumped towards him, looking with intense interest at Dacers' dishevelled appearance. His hat was gone, his dark topcoat was soiled with dust and dirt and his cravat was awry. 'I knew you were up to something when I saw you last night,' hooted Twells. 'I see by your condition that you were hardly taking a constitutional. What's been going on?'

'A little tidying up of the landscape, Amos — improving things rather in the spirit of Mr Bazalgette,' Dacers informed him brightly. Weariness from lack of sleep and his recent strenuous exertions had soaked into his very bones but he kept up a cocky front.

'Don't try to be humorous. And who were the two men who were with you a few minutes ago and who've now gone so quickly?'

'A pair of helpful gentlemen who gave a much appreciated hand in apprehending the two you see here. I think they had to dash away being late for an engagement,' Dacers stated without batting an eye. He hated evading the truth when dealing with his old friend from Scotland Yard but felt duty bound to protect the Bullochs from official scrutiny. He quickly changed the subject, nodding to Fortune, half dressed and shivering in the February cold and Tebbutt, both now being guarded by the foreman and some of his crew. 'I hand this pair over to you for reasons I'll explain later', he said. He lifted up the leatherwork false hump. 'And this object contains evidence vital to charges which will no doubt be brought.'

Again, he was holding back the full truth by not mentioning Sam Meakum who had disappeared but Meakum had moved to prevent Fortune and Tebbutt from killing him and, out of gratitude, he secretly hoped he would escape scot-free.

Twells' detective companions moved forward and placed their substantial hands on Fortune and Tebbutt.

Twells glowered at the pair of captives. 'Two rum looking coves, Septimus,' he rumbled. 'They ought to be displayed at the Egyptian Hall with the other curiosities. Are they Americans.'

'Yes. Why do you ask?'

Twells produced a folded paper from his pocket and handed it to Dacers.

'Because of this. A little urchin in rags and without shoes, looking as if he came out of the St. Giles Rookery or Seven Dials, rushed into the Detective Office just as I was finishing night duty and threw this on the desk. He said a bloke he didn't know gave him sixpence — a whole sixpence, if you don't mind — to deliver it. Then he ran off. It's because of this note that we came up here this morning.' Dacers unfolded the paper and perused it with his eyebrows raised in surprise. It read:

'*Inspector Twells, Sir:*

I am given to understand that there are some Americans in the region of the Blue Duck and Blindman's Yard, Hungerford Bridge, who're up to no good.

Mr. Septimus Dacers, whom I believe is known to you, has gone there alone in his professional capacity and I fear there is a good chance that he will be harmed by them. I respectfully suggest it would be in his best interests and the interests of the Queen's peace if your office investigated without delay. A Concerned Citizen.'

It was literate, written in the beautifully formed copperplate hand employed by engravers on legal documents and banknotes; there was a slight stain on one corner of the paper that looked like acid and the paper itself was of a kind recently handled by Dacers when he looked at a proof of the letterhead of the Resurgent South, alias the Dixie Ghosts.

Who'd have thought it? he commented mentally. *Setty Wilkins corresponding* with the 'crushers' he claims to hate! I felt all along he knew something about Fortune and his friends. The man's an enigma. He seems to know about everything. And he thought he heard the echo of Setty's archaic Cockney argot voicing something he had said a few days before:

'A man never knows vot's vot these days.'

Indeed he doesn't, Setty, old culley, assented Dacers mentally. Indeed he doesn't!

'Septimus, I want you to come with us and these beauties to Scotland Yard to provide information on them,' declared Amos Twells. 'We don't know the first thing about them or what their lurk is but I know you well enough to know you'd never collar them without proper cause.'

'A little later if you please, Amos,' said Dacers wearily. 'I'd like to have a couple of hours' sleep.'

Twells gave an irritated grunt. 'Oh, no! This is my case now and I want to be on firm ground from the first. You'll come now or I'll clap the darbies on you and drag you in.'

'Very well,' Dacers agreed with a sigh, 'but I hope you have the means of providing some tea and toast at the Detective Office.'

10

Just Deserts

At Scotland Yard, Septimus Dacers gave Twells a statement of what he knew of the activities of Fortune and his henchmen. It was a full disclosure but for the judicious omission of the true identities of James and Irvine Bulloch. There was no perversion of the course of justice in this for they played only a marginal role in the affair of the Dixie Ghosts. He described them as two unknown passers-by who helped in the capture of Fortune and Tebbutt.

The missing Sam Meakum was another matter since he had a material role in the group's attempts to obtain finances so Dacers gave information about him, emphasising the way he released Dacers when his murder was planned. Dacers hoped this would aid Meakum if he was brought to trial. Out of gratitude, he still secretly hoped Meakum managed to evade capture.

As he was on the way home after being at the headquarters of the detectives, he realised that, in spite of all the dizzying events that had occurred since he was plunged into the affair of the Dixie Ghosts, there was one glaring cause for dissatisfaction in the way it had turned out. He had not found the cause of Theodore Van Trask's troubles and therefore had not eased the distress of Roberta Van Trask, the bright-eyed and possibly naïve reason for his becoming involved in the first place. He had not fulfilled his promise to the girl.

Again, he felt that events had conspired to make a 'guy' of him.

And he was stabbed by a sword of guilt the moment he entered the door of his lodgings. Mrs. Slingsby was standing in the hall, looking grave and eyeing his crumpled and grubby appearance with a measure of alarm.

'Miss Van Trask is here, Mr. Dacers,' she said, 'And the poor girl seems very melancholy.'

As before, He found Roberta Van Trask seated in the parlour and she did indeed appear to be most distressed.

He apologised for his unshaven state and the condition of his clothing about which he felt acutely conscious in her presence. Then he apologised further. 'I'm sorry, Miss Van Trask. There have been many developments in my investigations since I agreed to assist you but I must admit I have so far failed to discover the reason for your father's unhappiness.' As he spoke, he had a haunting recollection of the scorning voice of Cal Tebbutt, known to Miss Van Trask as 'Fairfax' declaring in anything but the tones of a Virginia aristocrat that Theodore Van Trask had betrayed his country.

Her troubled face broke into a sad smile. 'That's all right, Mr. Dacers. I'm sure you have done your very best. I called again to tell you that something has happened to increase my father's worries. He has confided in me a little, but only a little and says that, more than ever, he is in danger of being disgraced. I fear the strain will bring on his earlier illness again and he is speaking of handing in his resignation to Mr. Adams.'

'What has happened to disturb him so?'

'A man, a Virginian, has shown up at the embassy and has asked for asylum. It seems he is frightened of the British authorities. He confesses to be an ex-Confederate but, as Mr. Lincoln said just before his death, we are one nation now. He is now a citizen of the United States and is entitled to asylum in the embassy.'

'And who is he?' asked Dacers.

'He says his name is Samuel Meakum.'

Dacers pricked up his ears at that. 'Does he? I happen to know something about him. Has he been given asylum?'

'Yes, but Mr. Adams says much depends on the nature of the reasons for which the British Crown wants him,' she said. 'There are some categories of law under which he must be handed over. He is lodged in the embassy for the time being until the legal staff can go into the matter. As soon as he arrived, my father became more worried. He has confided in me but it was only to say Meakum has the power to disgrace him — to ruin him. Nothing could induce him to say why. He is now on the verge of resigning and I'm sure it is through fear of this Meakum man revealing something damaging about him. I'm worried, Mr. Dacers. I do not want my father to be disgraced after all his years in diplomacy and I do not want him to resign if the matter is small but exaggerated in his mind by his state of anxiety.'

Again, Dacers recalled Tebbutt, snarling from under the seated James Bulloch that Theodore Van Trask was a traitor. Whatever knowledge Tebbutt had of that matter was obviously shared by Sam Meakum. It might be something that would shock Roberta Van Trask if it came to light, though she plainly wanted to know about it. He decided to say nothing to her about the allegation of treason so as not to worry her further but it now seemed imperative that he fulfil his original task on her behalf.

Prodded by the anxiety written on the face of Roberta Van Trask, his brain began to race, seeking a solution. He balanced what he knew of the characters of Theodore Van Trask; the American Ambassador, Charles Francis Adams and Sam Meakum. The first two were of proven stolid devotion to their duties as servants of their country with the exception, in Van Trask's case, of the flaw of an allegation of treasonable behaviour made by Tebbutt, a man of erratic and sometimes unbalanced temperament.

Meakum, with his blocky build and pugnacious face, looked like a prizefighter but was not so ruffianly as his appearance suggested. Dacers recalled his efforts to restrain Tebbutt when he tended to violent extremes but his crowning act in Dacers' eyes was his releasing of Dacers when he was on the very verge of being murdered then cutting himself loose from Fortune and Tebbutt. There was certainly decency in Sam Meakum.

Roberta Van Trask studied Dacers as he stood in front of her, dishevelled, tousle haired, dusty and looking anything but his usual well turned out self. He held his hand to his head, thinking deeply and she felt a lift of the heart and a surge of warm affection for him. He appeared to her a hero, battered and wearied by his recent misadventures but ready to champion her father and himself.

Dacers took his hand from his head and said: 'Miss Van Trask, what does Mr. Adams think of your father?'

She looked puzzled. 'Why, I know he has the greatest respect for him and the greatest trust in him. Both he and Mrs. Adams were extremely kind to him during his bout of illness.'

'And what does he think of me?'

'Well, I know he has a great deal of faith in you and he has told you himself how much he appreciated your help when you accompanied my father to Liverpool.'

'And, lastly, what does he feel about you?'

'He has always shown me the most tender affection. Mr. Adams is a family man and I always felt he was as kind to me as to his own children.'

Dacers' unshaven face relaxed into a slight smile. 'Good. So we are all in good standing with Mr. Adams. Do you think, if you make an overture on my behalf, he will allow me into the embassy to talk to Samuel Meakum in confidence? But do not let your father know about it under any circumstances.'

The girl frowned. 'I'm not sure. I don't know anything about the diplomatic niceties of such a thing but I will ask Mr. Adams if it is possible.'

'Good, but, remember, your father must know nothing about it. So, if I visit the embassy, I do not want to encounter Mr. Van Trask. You might suggest that Meakum and I meet at a secluded spot in the garden,' Dacers said.

'I'll try, Mr. Dacers,' she promised. 'I'll try'.

Her efforts were not in vain and, the following morning, a footman from the U.S. Embassy arrived at Dacers' lodgings with a formal note bringing the compliments of the Honourable Charles Francis Adams, United States' Ambassador to the Court of St. James, requesting the company of Septimus Dacers, Esq. the following afternoon. It specified that Mr. Dacers should meet Mr. Adams in the garden of the embassy.

Dacers, in sober frock coat, tall hat and carrying his stick, arrived at the embassy with some trepidation. He was going to take a chance on behalf of Theodore Van Trask and his daughter and hoped it would pay off. Everything depended on Sam Meakum co-operating with him and on the breadth of tolerance and understanding of Ambassador Adams.

Charles Francis Adams himself, gravely dignified in middle age with white hair on two sides of a balding portion of his head, met him in the vestibule of the building and offered his hand. 'Mr Dacers, welcome to the soil of the United States. I remember with gratitude your earlier service for us,' he greeted. 'Our guest, Mr. Meakum, is willing to see you and is waiting in the garden. I am sure there is no reason why you should not converse in private, so I'll take you to him and leave you alone.'

Sam Meakum, in new clothing obviously supplied by the Embassy and looking very different from the shaking, fearful man who cut Dacers' bonds, was sitting in a chair in a quiet corner of the garden. A second chair had been provided for Dacers.

They shook hands. 'First, I want to thank you for cutting me loose at Blindman's Yard and for saving me from a watery grave,' said Dacers. 'I want you to know that, if the British authorities claim you and the embassy cannot protect you, I'll speak up for you at your trial.'

Meakum looked relieved and mumbled his thanks.

'And, to save the reputation of a good man, I'd like to know exactly what hold Cal Tebbutt had over Mr. Van Trask and why he burst in on him and threatened him with a pistol.'

Meakum spoke volubly, seeming only too willing to unfold the story.

'Tebbutt and I hit hard times,' he began. 'I came from a Virginia farm but ran away to sea as a youngster to get away from my bullying old man. In the war between the States, I was in a Southern ship running the Yankee blockade on the Southern coast. That's where I met Tebbutt, likewise a Virginian who'd had a wandering time. He'd served in the Confederate Army from early in the war, got some kind of a head wound in the battle of Shiloh and it caused him to act kind of peculiar every once in a while, 'specially after drinking.

'Well, he was released from the army after being wounded and seems to have drifted around a bit then decided he'd try the sea. Though he was no kind of a sailor, the blockade running business needed all the hands it could get and he finished up in my ship, the *Possum*. I kind of took to him and helped him out so far as seamanship was concerned. He came to depend on me quite a bit. Then disaster struck us. We were running for Southampton to collect a cargo we hoped to break through the blockade with when a Yankee vessel trailed us and sank us.' Meakum paused and shuddered at the memory.

'Tebbut and me survived in the sea for a long time but many shipmates drowned. In the end, we were picked up by a British ship and brought into Southampton. We were stranded in England, had our fill of war and wandered a while, getting a little work here and there and we finally reached London.'

Meakum went on to tell how the pair discovered the Blue Duck. Josiah Tooley, the landlord, had a young brother who emigrated to America, settled in South Carolina and joined a state militia regiment at the beginning of the Civil War. He was killed early in the hostilities. This connection made Tooley sympathetic to the South and his pub became popular with various Southerners in London. A very mixed bag.

Through the Blue Duck, the pair of stranded seamen made contact with Henry Hotze. An energetic Swiss journalist who had earlier settled in Alabama, Hotze established a pro-Confederate newspaper, *The Index*, in London. It sought to bring British public opinion to accept the breakaway Southern states as a legitimate nation.

Meakum and Tebbutt began to work for him, distributing the paper and performing other chores. This brought them in some regular money, which, unfortunately, gave Tebbutt a chance to indulge in hard liquor. And, because he thought it would give him some standing among Southern exiles and the British upper crust, he adopted the distinguished name of Fairfax.

During their association with Hotze, the pair frequented the region of the United States' Embassy, monitoring the comings and goings there and occasionally picking up scraps of gossip and rumour useful to *The Index*'s campaign. One day, while in the small park near the embassy, they encountered Theodore Van Trask, taking the air. When speaking to Northeners in the vicinity of the embassy, they disguised their Southern accents as best they could and Van Trask, in conversation with them, seemed not to realise that they were Southerners.

Septimus Dacers leaned forward in his chair, eager for the part of Meakum's narrative he most wanted to hear.

An hour later, he was in the office of Charles Francis Adams, sitting before Adams' desk, having just related to Adams what Meakum told him. He had mixed feelings of both fear and hope. For he had taken a chance on either saving or ruining the diplomatic career of Theodore Van Trask as well as his reputation as an American loyal to the Union.

Adams leaned back in his chair and looked at Dacers levelly. 'So, Mr. Dacers,' he said, 'as a lawyer, I like to have a full grasp of the evidence. So, let me review everything I have heard from you.

'You say Mr Van Trask, on meeting Meakum and Tebbutt revealed to them that his nephew, Major Nicholas Van Trask, was a prisoner of the Confederates in Libby Prison in Richmond? Heaven knows that was a ghastly place, a converted tobacco warehouse where captured Union officers were housed in wretched conditions and half starved. Certainly, no man deserved to be held there, much less some of the best officers in the Union service.'

Ambassador Adams paused and his face reflected his disgust at the thought of Libby Prison. 'I knew from Mr Van Trask, of course, that his nephew was a prisoner in Richmond but understood he managed to escape. I did not know the details Meakum revealed: that he and Tebbutt told Mr. Van Trask that Hotze, that slippery but clever enemy of the Union, had influence with certain circles in Richmond and could organise the major's release for a sum of money — a considerable sum, which would go into the Confederate war coffers.

'Mr. Van Trask kept it all secret from his daughter and myself, met the pair in secret and paid over the money. Meakum and Tebbutt were honest brokers in that deal.'

Adams seemed slightly amused, shook his head and the suggestion of a smile passed over his lips. 'I'll say this for Henry Hotze: so far as my side in the war was concerned, he was a confounded nuisance, but an honest one according to his lights. The money went into the sources that saw to Major Van Trask's release. I can tell you that the major's story from then on was one of extreme heroism, though ultimately tragic.

'Now, as to this other matter at a later date, of which I was also ignorant. After the war, when funds from Hotze dried up, Tebbutt and Meakum fell in with the confidence trickster, Fortune and were gullible or hard up enough to join him in his Resurgent South scheme.

'Tebbutt, who liked to call himself Fairfax, when out with his henchman, and passing Mr. Van Trask's home, having had some hard liquor, was seized by the crazed notion that Mr. Van Trask owed him some personal remuneration for his services concerning the major, though none was promised. So he rushed in and threatened him with a pistol and demanded money. You tell me this caused Mr. Van Trask considerable mental anguish. Well, I'm only grateful that he came to no harm in the incident.'

The Ambassador rose, stretched his arm over his desk and offered Dacers his hand.

'Thank you, Mr. Dacers,' he said. 'Again, you have done a valuable service for us.'

'Thank you, Mr. Ambassador', Dacers replied. 'I only hope I have done the right thing by everyone concerned.'

Charles Francis Adams face became grave. 'On that point, I will exercise a lawyer's discretion, keep my own counsel and leave you to judge that at the end of the case, so to speak.'

Later that same evening, in the lamplit quiet of the Ambassador's office an earnest conversation went on between Charles Francis Adams and Theodore Van Trask.

'No. no,' protested Van Trask, 'I can only resign. I gave aid to our enemy. It was at a time when I had been ill and perhaps my judgement was weakened but that will not do. It is a feeble excuse. No man should betray his country in time of war. I can only resign. I have disgraced not only myself but the name of Van Trask. You know my family served the nation honourably ever since its founding.'

'Resign? Disgraced?' exclaimed Adams. 'I can't agree, Theodore. You might have contributed to the rebel states but it was the merest pittance compared to the vast amounts in money and in subsequent damage to the United States' fighting forces made by those people in this country who financed and built the Confederate commerce raiders and rams. And consider what you achieved. You caused Major Van Trask to be freed from festering in the hell hole of Libby Prison and return to where he was most useful to his country — the field of battle.

'You know I have a son who is an officer in our army. Do you think I would not be tempted to do the same thing as you if I heard he was a captive in Libby Prison?

'Look at the end result. Major Van Trask was killed in that terrible twelve day battle at Spotsylvania Court House and it is a matter of record that he and the men he led distinguished themselves to the very end. In his despatches, General Grant wrote in the most glowing and admiring terms of the leadership of your nephew and the bravery of his troops.'

Adams put a firm, encouraging hand on Van Trask's shoulder. 'Theodore, my old friend, if you made a mistake, it was made out of affection for your brother

216

and his son and far worse mistakes have been made than providing the means of returning a gallant and valuable officer to the work of defending the Union. You have long been as valuable to our diplomatic service and to me personally as your nephew was to the flag of the nation. I will not hear of your resignation.'

Still with one hand on Van Trask's shoulder, Adams clamped his other hand on the opposite shoulder, shook Van Trask gently and said: 'And if you dared to offer your resignation, I would chain you to your desk and insist on your continuing your duties. The matter is closed, my dear Theodore.'

As to the Resurgent South trio, the wheels of the law took their usual slow time in measuring out just deserts the weight of which fell heaviest on Fortune who was convicted for conspiracy to murder. Additionally, he was found to be the only one to make any concrete profit from the group's scheming for it was proved that, when supposedly pursuing business on his solo trips away from his colleagues, he was attending to the salting away for his own use such profits as was made by their trickery. For that, he was convicted for obtaining money by deception and was given a total sentence of fifteen years in a convict prison with deportation to the United States at the end of it.

Calvin Tebbutt, judged an accomplice in the conspiracy to murder and on the deception charge, from which he made no profit, received a total of eight years in prison to be followed by deportation.

Samuel Meakum was found to be amenable to the British law and handed over by the United States' Embassy. Septimus Dacers, who came so close to being a murder victim, appeared as a character witness for him and described how his life was certainly saved when Meakum freed him at Blindman's Yard. This told well in Meakum's favour and he was imprisoned for two years for being an accomplice in attempting to obtain money by deception. In his case, there was no recommendation of deportation.

The few British dupes gullible enough

to give Fortune's pockets a temporarily golden lining in the belief that they were stacking up future profits from a revitalised Confederate States and who were forced to give evidence, quickly bolted to their retreats to hide their red faces. They included Sir Oswald Vaillant, the Squire of Cardsworth, who had invested in the fantasy of an improved version of Hunley's undersea boat.

Well before the bewigged majesty of the law courts balanced the Dixie Ghosts miscreants on the scales of justice, in fact the day after Charles Francis Adams' warm-hearted interview with Theodore Van Trask, another letter for Dacers arrived at his address. It was handed to him by Mrs. Slingsby, wearing a smile that might be described as one of fond conjecture. For the note was addressed in a feminine hand she had seen before and she wondered if a succession of such letters might ultimately lead to the 'nice wife' she hoped he would find.

In the letter, Roberta Van Trask recorded her heartfelt gratitude for the service Dacers performed for her father and herself. It had resulted in a heavy burden being lifted from her father's shoulders and he was working at his diplomatic duties with the sort of vigour he must have had when a young man, new to the service.

A couple of days later, Dacers walked down Little Earle Street to enter the heart of Seven Dials. His mood was light. He was deaf to the wailings of babies and the exchanges of lurid bawling between couples who might or might not have been united in Holy Matrimony. He scarcely smelt the harsh and sickly stench of stewing hops from the big brewery, dominating Castle Street, on the further side of 'The Dials'. He even gave twopence each to four small ragged boys and was spared the usual siege by a horde of their kind with grubby palms open and pitiful pleas for a 'brown.' meaning a penny.

At Setty Wilkins' workshop, he handed the ancient engraver a paper on which he had inscribed a legend.

Setty read it and his wrinkled, gnome's face split into a grin.

Dacers said: 'Setty Wilkins, who claims to have no book learning and who produces literate messages in an immaculate copperplate that even Inspectors of crushers can understand, I want one copy of this on the choicest grade of card you have in the shop. Oh, and please be sure it is unmarred by an acid stain.'

Setty read the paper again, chuckled and took the clay pipe from his mouth.

'My eye, Mr. Dacers,' he pronounced, 'I don't know vot you mean and I allus thought you vos the perfect bachelor but, as I've often remarked, a man never knows vot's vot these days!'

The paper declared that, at an early forthcoming date:

'*Septimus Dacers, Esq, has pleasure in requesting the company of Miss Roberta Van Trask and Chaperone for a little dinner at Carrington's Hotel, St. James' Place. RSVP.*'

We do hope that you have enjoyed reading this large print book.

Did you know that all of our titles are available for purchase?

We publish a wide range of high quality large print books including:

Romances, Mysteries, Classics
General Fiction
Non Fiction and Westerns

Special interest titles available in large print are:

The Little Oxford Dictionary
Music Book, Song Book
Hymn Book, Service Book

Also available from us courtesy of Oxford University Press:

Young Readers' Dictionary
(large print edition)
Young Readers' Thesaurus
(large print edition)

For further information or a free brochure, please contact us at:
Ulverscroft Large Print Books Ltd.,
The Green, Bradgate Road, Anstey,
Leicester, LE7 7FU, England.
Tel: (00 44) 0116 236 4325
Fax: (00 44) 0116 234 0205

DEADLY MEMOIR

Ardath Mayhar

When Margaret Thackrey, ex-government agent and writer, decides to pen her memoirs, she unwittingly gets the attention of a vicious assassin — a man whose nefarious deeds she'd nearly uncovered during her service. Now he must stop the publication of her book before his true character is revealed. He murders Margaret's husband, and stalks her from Oregon to Texas, where she must finally confront her past — and a determined, stone-cold killer!

THE GRAB

Gordon Landsborough

In Istanbul, a beautiful girl is grabbed from her hotel bed and taken out into the night. But Professional Trouble-Buster Joe P. Heggy is looking on and decides to investigate: who was the girl and why was she kidnapped? But when thugs try to eliminate him, he is equal to their attempts, especially when he's aided by a bunch of American construction workers. Then things get very tense when Heggy finds the girl — and then kidnaps her himself . . .

THE PURPLE GLOVE MURDERS

Mary W. Burgess

In Southern California, Gail Brevard and her law partner Conrad 'Connie' Osterlitz are relaxing at their mountain hideaway. When retired Justice Winston Craig is found dead, face down on Black Bear Lake, Gail is asked to find the cause of his death. She becomes convinced it is linked to one of his old cases. However, when Connie is attacked and lies near death, Gail must use all her resources to solve the crime before it's too late . . .

A HEART THAT LIES

Steve Hayes and Andrea Wilson

Jackie O'Hara has been in a race against time. Terminally ill, she's determined to make peace with her estranged brother, yet there is just one problem — first, she must find him. Meanwhile, Danny is being chased by the Russian Mafia who want him dead, and Interpol, who need him to testify against mob boss Dmitri Kaslov. That makes Jackie a target as well, because they all hope she will lead them straight to him . . .